Wedding Dreams

(Second in Rescue Me Saga Extras)

Kallypso Masters

Wedding Dreams
Second in Rescue Me Saga Extras
Kallypso Masters

Copyright © 2019
Ka-thunk! Publishing
Print Edition
E-book ISBN: 978-1941060346
Print ISBN: 978-1941060353

Original e-book version: May 20, 2019
Original print version: May 20, 2019

ALL RIGHTS RESERVED
WEDDING DREAMS
Content edited by Meredith Bowery
Line edited by Jacy Mackin
Cover design by Linda Kuhlmann of Two Trees Studio
Cover images licensed through Shutterstock
and graphically altered by Linda Kuhlmann
Formatted by BB eBooks

To discover more about the books in this series, see the Books by Kallypso Masters page at the end of this book. For more about Kallypso Masters, please go to the About the Author section.

Dedication

To Sara and Craig,
may all your wedding dreams come true
and married life be filled with countless blessings.

Acknowledgements

It takes a village to get one of my novels to the point of being "ready." I had so much help from my readers in the Rescue Me Saga Discussion Group on Facebook. I'd like to especially recognize by name the readers of Italian descent who shared scenarios for how the wedding planning, ceremony, and reception could go down for Marc and Angelina. My thanks to Marianne Chiumento (Kitty Angel, Guilty Pleasures BR), Tammy Lenze, Kristen M., Gina Marcantonio, and Maria Palma for sharing your delightful stories. Of course, I always pick and choose, blend, and add my own dramatic flair, but you helped me see how reality looks.

As Marc embarks on his new career as an EMT, I also enlisted the help of Patryce Cornett, a fan and the wife (/manager!) of her firefighter/EMT hubby, Michael Cornett FF/NRP/FP-C. I first approached Patryce on Facebook for help with my Raging Fire series about Angelina's firefighter brothers, the first novel of which I started serializing monthly this past March on the Patreon app as I'm writing it. (NOTE: Those who prefer a completed novel will get to read each professionally edited novel when they're ready starting in 2020.) For Marc, as well as Tony and Rafe Giardano, Patryce helped me flesh out work schedules and an organizational chart for the fictional Aspen Corners Fire Department for these overlapping series. The amount of effort you put into the questions for that EMT college in Colorado, plus follow-up phone calls, Patryce, amazed me! Thanks so much and welcome to my team!

To my loyal, long-suffering, and totally awesome beta readers, especially Barb Jack and Lisa Simo-Kinzer, who never cease to amaze me in how many times you will reread my manuscripts to help me get them right and avoid new problems with each iteration.

Patryce Cornett also came on board to beta read this one after I found her in connection with my first serial novel, *Tony: Slow Burn* (Raging Fire #1).

And thanks also to those of you who gave the early-early beta drafts of *Wedding Dreams* a read and helped shape the direction of the story in ways big and small—Margie Dees, Tammy Lenze, Gina Marcantonio, and Carmen Messing. Thank you *all* so much for giving of your time and effort.

To my content editor, Meredith Bowery, who helps me stay consistent within my Rescue Me Saga world and keep my timeline straight, and provides incredible insights into my characters whom she seems to know as if they were friends. And to Jacy Mackin, my line editor, who never lets me put out a sloppy book and challenges me when necessary to make it better.

To my proofreaders—Annette Elens and Christine Mulcair—for going over the final manuscript with fine-tooth combs and for polishing it to its shiniest. I'd be terrified to put out anything without you having one last look, Christine, and am happy to have Annette on board again for pre-publishing proofreading!

To my amazing cover artist, Linda Kuhlmann, who has been with me since 2011. I'll miss you after you retire in July, but your amazing covers will keep my books hopping off book shelves forever!

Chapter One

"Let's elope."

Angelina tuned out their politely bickering family members sitting face-to-face across the six-foot round table. The quiet corner of her new restaurant, La Casetta, in Breckenridge had been the perfect place to meet on a slow Wednesday afternoon in late October. If only their deliberations had been so perfect.

Suddenly, Marc's words registered. She turned to him, leaned in, and whispered, "What did you say?"

He nodded toward their family members, keeping his voice low as well. "This is turning into a circus. They no longer give a damn what either of us wants. I say we elope and get on with the honeymoon and our married life together. We can put the money we save into the house."

Marc was right, but elope? She couldn't deprive her mother of giving Angelina the wedding both had dreamed of but was beginning to think it was more about their mamas' wishes than it was about what Marc and Angelina wanted.

Each family was firmly entrenched on their own half of the table. Marc's mother and sister, Carmella, sat to his right while Angelina's mother and brother Tony were on her left. She'd invited Rafe, who'd agreed to help Mama with wedding costs as the current patriarch of the Giardano family. When his shift at the fire station had kept him away today, Tony agreed to fill in. He'd wound up sitting next to Carmella as the two families circled the wagons. The two barely acknowledged one another. They'd definitely gotten off on the wrong foot last year when Angelina had called Tony to pick her up after a misunderstanding with Marc. Sparks had flown between them that night at the café, too.

But if the two families couldn't agree on more at this second planning session, they'd never progress to more important issues, like what size guest list each family would be limited to. So far, they'd disagreed on everything from the table decorations to the time of day for the ceremony to whether they'd have Jordan almonds as guest favors, plus so many other trivial matters. This latest round of negotiations was going nowhere fast.

Had everyone lost sight of the goal here—ushering Marc and Angelina into marriage? Before Angelina could bring the discussion back to where it needed to be—on reception plans—Mama asked if she'd consider increasing the size of her bridal party.

"Your cousin Martina would make a beautiful bridesmaid. After all, she's flying all the way from Sicily."

She hadn't seen Martina in over a decade! Besides, both she and Marc had commitments from all their attendants.

"Mama, we talked about this months ago. I'll be attended by Carmella,"—she smiled across the table at her soon-to-be sister-in-law—"and my friends Karla, Savannah, Cassie, and Pippa."

While Carmella was the only one related to her or Marc by blood, Angelina had invited her family of choice first. When Marc added Tony at Angelina's request, he had one more attendant than she did. She'd thought immediately of Pippa Trapani, her sous-chef, whom Angelina had spent more time with in the last year than she had Marc. The two had become good friends in the process of opening and running Angelina's small Italian restaurant. Pippa had been thrilled to be included. And, with the establishment closing down for several days around the time of the wedding, Angelina was happy she'd have someone she could trust to run things while she was off on her honeymoon.

In addition to Tony as a groomsman, Marc had asked his

brother Sandro and his military brother Damián, as well as his former search-and-rescue partner, Luke. Adam would be his best man. They wanted symmetry and had limited it to their closest friends and family members. There was absolutely no reason to add anyone else to the wedding party at this stage.

Before Angelina could address Mama's disappointment over Martina, though, Marc's mother asked, "Did you see the children who attended Kate Middleton at her wedding to Prince William last year? Those darling bridesmaids and page boys were delightful."

Marc and Angelina barely knew any young boys and girls and had decided on Damián's nephew, José, and daughter, Marisol, to fulfill those roles. "I've already chosen everyone who will be in the wedding party, Mama D. It's all settled. All but two will be adults."

"What about having you delivered to the church in a horse and buggy?" Tony offered. "I'm sure Matt could provide both."

"Oh, I'm sure Angelina would prefer to go to the church in a Cinderella coach to marry her handsome prince," Mama D said, smiling toward Marc.

"I don't think there are any Cinderella coaches in Aspen Corners, Mama D'Alessio." She felt more comfortable reining in her own mother, rather than her future mother-in-law, but she wanted to nip that in the bud now.

How were they going to arrive at an affordable wedding when they went off on such fantastic tangents? Neither family listened to her and Marc's wishes, nor each other. Why couldn't their families agree on anything? Perhaps they should have intermingled their families more since they'd announced their engagement, but they'd been too busy working and overseeing the building of their new home.

Her head pounded with what had become the mother of all headaches. Angelina rubbed her fingers between her eyes, trying to release the tension that had been building up since everyone had arrived for this late-lunch meeting. Marc's mom meant well, but the disparity in her family's ability to pay for what she wanted put unfair pressure on Angelina's family.

"You and Marc could ride off in the buggy after the reception to my house." Mama hadn't been sold on the fancy coach idea, apparently. "You can leave your vehicle there and head off on your honeymoon."

Conversation continued to buzz around her, but she was mentally spent.

"What do you say?" Marc whispered, stroking her thigh gently. He had to be aware of her stress level. "We can call them off here and now and find a little wedding chapel somewhere."

"You tempt me, but I can't, Marc. This wedding means too much to Mama. I'm her only daughter. When the boys marry, it will be up to the families of their brides to make the plans and foot the bill. This is her one shot at giving a daughter a wedding."

"We can pay for our own wedding and do it our way."

"I know, and we *will* pay for a lot of things, but Mama's been saving money for my wedding since she saw me in my First Communion veil and dress."

He grinned, bending close to her ear to whisper, "I'd like to see those photos. A preview of the big day."

"Let's hope my wedding dress will be a bit more mature."

"And revealing." His hand stroked down her back, but he groaned, probably because he was inhibited by too much fabric. "Perhaps with an open back like the one you wore at daVinci's that first night we danced."

"I've waited too late to have a custom design with only eight months until the wedding. The restaurant has kept me so busy, but I have several *Say Yes to the Dress* salon appointments in Denver the first Saturday in November. Hopefully, I'll find the perfect one on my first day trying."

"I'm going to love seeing you come down the aisle to stand by my side and speak your vows in whatever you choose to wear—but

I'll love even more removing the dress from your delicious body on our wedding night."

"Angelina, dear, what do you think of that idea?" Mama D asked.

What on earth had her future mother-in-law just asked her? She needed to stop fantasizing about Marc undressing her and pay closer attention to this conversation. What she thought about having her son undress her? Heat infused her cheeks as she turned toward the woman and smiled weakly. Why she was embarrassed, when Mama D knew the two of them had lived together since the spring, was puzzling.

Marc came to her rescue. "Which idea in particular, Mama? It's hard to keep up."

"About having the wedding and reception at the resort."

Angelina turned toward her mother, who appeared to be biting the inside of her lower lip to keep her temper in check.

"While I'm sure that would make for a beautiful venue, I don't think so, Mama D'Alessio," Angelina began. "I've always pictured myself being married in my family church in Aspen Corners." She had fantasized about her own wedding dreams since childhood.

Mama relaxed somewhat at her words, and Angelina decided she needed to hold her ground on this point, if no other.

"But I'm afraid the church hall and even the church itself won't be large enough to accommodate both of our guest lists," Mama D'Alessio said.

"Angelina wants to have her wedding in *our home church*," Tony insisted rather harshly. While she appreciated him for speaking up, his lack of finesse in dealing with Mama D's feelings made Angelina cringe inwardly.

Carmella bristled, glaring at him at first then turning toward Angelina and dismissing him. "Are there any larger venues in Aspen Corners?"

She tried to think of a bigger venue, but nothing came to mind.

Mama cleared her throat before Angelina could respond. "There have been huge weddings in our church for more than a century—some with two hundred or more guests. And everyone *fit* into the hall." Mama's voice had taken on a defensive edge as she glared at Marc's mother. This dual family meeting was deteriorating rapidly. Angelina needed to fix this.

While Angelina tried to figure out how, Mama D continued, "I'm sure that's fine for a small-town wedding, but this one will be twice that size. Maybe larger."

"It will?" Angelina asked, her lunch souring in her stomach as she thought what this would mean for Mama's bank account. Just who were all these long-lost relatives and friends they insisted on inviting? She thought the D'Alessios only had a few relatives in America when they arrived with Marc as a young man. Marc's Gramps—a World War II Marine taken in and cared for by Mama D's mother after being wounded in a battle in the Apennines of Northern Italy—for sure. How big could the man's family be, and did Marc know them well?

"Papa and I have many friends who must be there as well," Mama D chimed in, "and would feel slighted if not invited."

Her and Marc's preliminary list had consisted of only eighty or so people. It seemed they were about to be invaded by dozens, if not hundreds, of people she and Marc didn't even know.

Carmella interjected, almost apologetically, "Our list is about two hundred and thirty, including plus ones. Some of them are business acquaintances, but most are friends of the family and Gramps's extended family, many of whom live here in Colorado." Marc had told her Gramps was the reason the D'Alessios had settled in Colorado in the first place. "Of course, not all who are invited would be expected to attend."

But what if they did all come? Angelina refused to let Mama go into debt over this one-day event. In Italian families, it was still traditional for the bride's family to pay for the reception.

"Please go over your list again." Squaring her shoulders, Angelina continued, "Limit it to about one hundred, not counting the ones we already have on our list, so that everyone will fit in the church and at the reception."

"Mama," Marc began, "we were hoping for something more intimate with family and friends anyway. I'm sure you understand."

Thank God he'd spoken up, because no way could Angelina accommodate that many people, no matter where it was held. She wanted to make homemade pasta and bake the traditional cookies that would be given to guests at the reception and to take home as favors.

Mama D waved away her son's concern. "This will be the wedding of the century. You can't restrict that to just a small group."

Even Prince William and Kate Middleton had capped how many attended their wedding and receptions.

"Our family is loved and respected," Mama D continued. Almost as an afterthought, she added, "Both of our families, of course."

"I want to be married in my family church," Angelina said firmly. That was nonnegotiable.

"We have family coming all the way from Sicily," her mama said, making eye contact with no one in particular. "Between my siblings and my late husband's family, all of whom will want to be at the wedding, we could have that many as well, Angelina. We can have additional chairs placed in the side aisles to accommodate more guests."

"Honestly, Mama, you don't think our business associates will care anything about the wedding ceremony," Carmella said. She turned to Angelina. "What if we do separate invitations for the reception than for the ceremony and keep the wedding small and intimate and in your church, but hold the reception at Bella Montagna?"

"Guests from Aspen and Denver wouldn't mind waiting on the

wedding party to arrive at the resort if we held a cocktail hour for them," Mama D added.

Angelina's dream of an intimate church wedding seemed safe at the moment, but how would her family be able to afford the wedding of the century and the monstrous price tag that would accompany it?

Once again, things were getting out of hand.

"Of course, the D'Alessio family would pick up the tab for that cocktail party. Right, Mama?" Carmella asked.

"Absolutely."

"The Giardano family will be paying for the reception after the wedding," Tony chimed in. "Wherever it is. Sis, how about Breckenridge for the reception?"

Breckenridge would have plenty of places for a crowd that size, but if they were going to hold a lavish reception, where better than at Marc's family resort? However, did she want the guests attending the wedding to have to drive an hour to get to Aspen and the reception? Breckenridge was only twenty minutes away but not nearly as connected to their families. What should she do?

Angelina glanced up at Marc, who looked miserable, too. "We could do separate invitations," she suggested. "Family and close friends will be invited to the wedding, while the other guests would only receive invitations to the reception."

Angelina's stomach churned again at having to decide who among her friends would be reception only. How else could they please both sides of the family, though? At the moment, Marc's idea about eloping sounded like their best solution.

Still, how could she trample her family's dreams or budget? "Mama, what are you most comfortable with?"

She patted Angelina's hand. "Whatever will make you happiest, my Angel."

Angelina turned to Marc. "Why don't we discuss this in private and come back and let them know our decision next week?" She hated making decisions like this, certain that whatever she chose would displease someone.

Marc leaned closer and whispered in her ear, *"Amore,* I don't want you stressing a minute longer. Whatever we agree to, we'll make sure everything important to us is a part of our special day."

Angelina trusted him to make that happen. "You know what we want," she whispered back. "Tell them."

Marc smiled at her before focusing his attention on the others at the table. "Angelina wants to be married in her church surrounded by a select group of friends and family in a more intimate ceremony." Angelina breathed a sigh of relief knowing that would be where she walked down the aisle toward the man of her dreams.

Both their mothers nodded, his somewhat more reluctantly. Tony and Carmella merely smiled.

Before anyone could say anything, he continued. "And we'll open up the reception to a larger group, but no more than four hundred guests. Mama Giardano, if you're in agreement, we can hold it at the resort, with the D'Alessios picking up the tab for a cocktail hour held before the wedding party arrives. The Giardanos will be in charge of the reception, and I'm sure Carmella and Sandro will agree to extend the family discount."

"Absolutely!" Carmella agreed. "I wouldn't hear of anything else. The meal and drinks at cost and no charge for the ballroom rental." As co-manager of the resort, she had the authority to make that decision.

That should make the family budget stretch much further.

"That would be fantastic, Carmella," Angelina said but wanted to be sure her mama and Tony found it acceptable. "How does that sound to you both?"

"Wonderful, baby," Mama said.

"The Giardanos don't need any handouts," Tony argued, narrowing his gaze at Carmella. "We'll pay the same price everyone else would."

Angelina rolled her eyes. Why did men have to be so pigheaded? They were close to reaching a consensus. Surely Rafe would be happy as long as she and Mama were happy.

She'd talk with Marc and Carmella later on to make sure the reception tab was discounted to make it closer to what her family could afford without hurting anyone's feelings. She smiled up at Marc, who nodded as if he knew her inmost thoughts.

He continued, "If we need to transport large numbers of guests between the resort and the church, we'll rent buses. Then we won't have to worry about anyone driving home after drinking too much."

What a great idea! Marc had been paying more attention to details than even she'd been aware of.

Marc stood and helped Angelina to her feet, effectively bringing this planning session to a close. "Now, if you'll excuse us, Angelina and I need to audition a band for the reception."

They had no such appointment scheduled, but Angelina wanted to get away as much as he did. As early as they could manage their schedules, Marc would be richly rewarded with the best blowjob she'd ever given him.

Chapter Two

Angelina looked at the racks and racks of dresses, completely overwhelmed. Karla and Savannah had pointed out numerous dresses they liked on the hangers but not on Angelina. Megan had taken so many photos of dresses Angelina would never see again that her delete finger was going to be sore. Carmella seemed to love anything Angelina came out in, but perhaps her mind was on getting back to the resort.

Mama, on the other hand, didn't care for anything that didn't have lace up to and surrounding her neck. Mama had no problem saying no to the dresses. She'd already nixed five in this salon—before Angelina had even gotten out of the dressing room—on top of the dozens of dresses she'd shot down in the other two boutiques they'd been in today.

Angelina's primary goal was to please Marc, but she didn't want to disappoint Mama while doing so. However, with a June wedding, no way did she want long sleeves and a Victorian high neckline. Marc thought she had a sexy neck, and she planned on wearing her hair up to show it off.

How was she going to please both of them while also finding a dress she loved?

"Oh, Angie, you have got to try on this one!" Karla said, showing her a lace-covered dress with three-quarter sleeves and a sweetheart neckline. The scalloped lace on the neck shimmered with beautiful beadwork giving it some sparkle without being gaudy. The bodice was perhaps a little lower cut than Mama's opinion of what was decent. She prepared herself to have yet another dress rejected.

"Let's take you back and try it on," the showroom attendant said, undoubtedly seeing Angelina's enthusiasm already starting to wane. When Mama stood to join them, Amanda turned to add, "Ladies, have a seat and enjoy some refreshments. We'll be right back so you can see the bride in the next dress." Out of earshot of the others, Amanda turned to Angelina and said, "You look like you needed a little break from the crowd."

Angelina stared at Amanda, her mouth having dropped open. "How did you know? My frustration wasn't too obvious, was it? I'd hate to hurt anyone's feelings."

Amanda laughed, shaking her head as she opened the door to the dressing room. After hanging the gown on the hook, she stroked Angelina's upper arm comfortingly, keeping her from working herself into a panic. "Not at all! I'm in awe of your patience, in fact. But trust me. I see this daily. Everyone comes in excited and hopeful, but the entourage tends to follow their own preferences. After the bride tries on a few dresses, she starts to lose her vision of what she wanted in the first place."

"I'm not sure I know what I want at this point. But I really need to find my dress today, if possible. I'd hate to tie everyone up for more shopping at such a busy time of year, but this is my last appointment."

"It's hard to know what you like when everyone has a different opinion about what she thinks is perfect on you."

Angelina had thought she'd found *the one* multiple times until Mama or someone else in her entourage had shot each one down.

"Don't let time pressure you to settle. I don't have any more appointments after yours, if you'd like to keep trying on more dresses. We don't close until seven." That was almost two hours away, longer than her original appointment.

"I really appreciate this, Amanda."

"No worries. Now let's see if we can find what you and Marc will love. What do you think he would want to see you in?"

"I'm sure he'll love anything." *Or nothing at all, more precisely.* Suddenly, she remembered their conversation at the planning session last month. "Do you have anything with a keyhole back?"

"Absolutely! In fact, the one Karla pulled for you does."

"Really?"

Amanda flipped the dress around on the hook, and for the first time, Angelina saw the expansive keyhole that would expose most of her back. This one revealed even more than the dress she'd worn to daVinci's the night she'd found Marc again. A tingle went down her spine as she imagined his hand pressing low against her back while they danced.

"Marc would love that!"

Amanda pointed toward the chair near the small table. "Before we try it on, I want you to sip some water. Take a breath."

Angelina responded easily to the familiar commands as her gaze fell on the dress hanging across the small room. She already could picture herself walking down the aisle and twirling around the dance floor in Marc's arms with that dress on.

"Ready to try on Karla's choice?"

Angelina stood, removed her robe and lifted her arms to have the dress lowered over her head and down her body. Unlike some she'd tried on earlier, this bodice fit like a glove and molded her girls perfectly. It would hardly need any alterations if she ordered this size. With a five-month estimated delivery time on the dress, she wouldn't have time for extensive alterations.

"I wish my bras fit this comfortably."

"It really is a one-of-a-kind fit, and you can have some alterations done if you wish. Maybe switch to cap or long sleeves when you order it from the designer."

"Oh, no! These are just right for a June wedding. I get hot easily." Especially with Marc around; he'd told her he'd be wearing his sexy dinner dress uniform that day.

"Let's hook you up in the back for the full effect." Amanda fastened the bodice just below the nape of her neck and flounced out the fit-and-flare skirt. When she stepped away from the mirror, Angelina got her first look.

She took it all in. Everything inside her told Angelina this was her dress.

"Breathe, Angelina."

She expelled a nervous laugh before taking a deep breath but never took her eyes off her reflection in the mirror.

The dress hugged her hourglass curves and made her hips look sexy, not wide. Tears flooded her eyes, which hadn't happened with any other dress she'd tried on today. She accepted the tissue Amanda held out to her. "It's weird to be crying and feeling like you're floating on air at the same time. This dress is beautiful."

"You're an absolute vision in it."

Her eyes stung as she whispered, "It's everything I dreamed of—and so much more."

"Trust me. When they see how hard you've fallen for this gown, the rest of them are going to be in love with it, too." Amanda's assurances helped drain away any lingering panic Angelina felt.

Angelina dabbed at her eyes so she could take a closer look then swiveled to see the back, one of her best assets. The keyhole bared her from the lower shoulder blades then tapered to a low vee just above the base of her spine. From there, a row of buttons covered in the same material as the dress extended over her ass down to where the skirt flared out about mid-thigh.

"Are those buttons functional or only an illusion?"

"They're completely functional. If you'd prefer, we can replace the covered buttons with pearl ones."

"No, these are perfect." Those buttons were as suggestive as hell. "Marc is so going to love stripping me out of this dress."

Amanda laughed. "I'm sure he will. That's probably the favorite part about wedding dresses for most grooms."

Angelina swished the lace-covered, flared skirt as she shimmied her hips back and forth. The dress made her feel sexy and princess-like all at once.

"So gorgeous! Not only the dress, but I feel gorgeous wearing it."

"It's a fabulous look on you, Angelina." Amanda picked up the veil they'd chosen because it most closely resembled Mama's. "I know you plan to use your mother's veil on your big day, but let's put this one on before we go out to *wow* your mama and friends."

"Sorry I left mine at home," Angelina apologized. She'd been solely focused on finding a dress, not on how it would look with Mama's veil. "But the veil might hide some of the back so my Mama can get beyond the expanse of flesh I'll be displaying."

One thing was certain, though. Mama's veil would be ditched after Mass, because Angelina wanted to show off her back in this gown at the reception. She'd have her hair in an updo with flowers or something that wouldn't be mussed by the veil. Something easy to undo on her wedding night so she could feel his hands in her hair the moment they stepped into their honeymoon suite. Marc loved having her hair cascading down her back.

"We want them to get the full effect from the first time they see you in this gown, because you're absolutely glowing. And this type of veil will be perfect," Amanda said as she attached a cathedral-length veil with blusher to the back of Angelina's head, below the haphazard bun. Amanda stepped back to check everything out, untucking some of the scalloped lace in the neckline.

Angelina did a half-twirl and checked out the back view again. "With the veil, the dress is demure enough for Mama to find acceptable inside the church, but then anything goes when Marc sees this back after I remove the veil for the reception."

"Absolutely stunning. Are we ready to let them know you've found your dress?"

Taking a deep breath, she nodded. She'd let no one convince her this wasn't her dress. Holding up the skirt so it wouldn't drag, she followed Amanda back to the showroom.

"Here comes our bride, ladies!" she announced. "And she's found her dress!"

"Angie! I knew the minute I saw that dress that it would be perfect for you!"

Megan snapped photos for the wedding story album. Savannah covered her mouth, speechless, but her eyes were bright with unshed tears. Finally, she whispered, "It's so perfect on you."

"My brother is going to be blown away when he sees you, Angelina," Carmella said.

"I know! I feel like it was made just for me!" Angelina had purposely not looked at Mama yet so as not to burst her euphoria, but the silence from that end of the couch was deafening. Turning toward Mama, she couldn't believe tears were streaming down her mother's face.

Did that mean she hated it or loved it? Angelina held her breath. Her eyes welled up again when Mama smiled through her tears and said, "I wish Papa was here to see you."

That did it. The dam exploded, and she found herself seated next to Mama, hugging her as both of them cried for who would be missing out on her wedding day. She hadn't longed to see Papa this much in such a long time. After dreaming of having him walk her down the aisle since she was a little girl, the reality hit hard that she could never have that dream fulfilled.

When she thought she would be able to control her emotions again, Angelina pulled away and searched Mama's face. "So you love it, too, Mama?"

Unable to speak yet, she nodded vigorously before clearing her throat. "It is perfect in every way. You're going to be the most beautiful bride, Angelina."

Mama hadn't seen the revealing back yet, but no need to put a damper on this moment. Besides, nothing Mama might say to the negative would change her mind. Resolute and without waiting to be asked the question familiar to everyone who watched the popular show, Angelina turned her head towards Amanda, keeping her back from Mama's gaze, and said, "I'm saying *yes* to the dress!"

A chorus of cheers erupted in the showroom, and she hugged Mama, her bridesmaids, and her matron of honor when she heard a champagne cork pop. Everyone turned to find Amanda pouring a flute of bubbly for each of them.

It had been a grueling day between three salons, but for it to end with her finding the dress she would wear as she walked down the aisle toward Marc made it all worthwhile. The next seven-and-a-half months couldn't pass fast enough, even if she did still have so much to get done.

"Now that we have *my* dress taken care of, how about we look at some dress styles for you girls?" Turning to the attendant, she asked, "Amanda, can you show us some tea-length styles available in teal or turquoise?" Angelina asked.

"Absolutely! I have several. Although not all of them are in your colors, we can order them in plenty of time."

They probably wouldn't all be able to get together again before the rehearsal given everyone's busy lives and the fact that Savannah's baby was due in January and her father's trial started next month.

"As long as you promise I won't have my final fitting until March or April," Savannah said, patting her belly, "after delivering this baby and losing any unwanted weight during the months after my little one's birth."

Maybe dress shopping would distract Savannah from worrying about everything coming up in her life. Angelina hated that she'd have to testify against that monster in her condition—hell, in any condition it would be horrific.

"That will be plenty of time, Savannah," Amanda said. "Just let me know what size to order it in, and we'll hook you up with a seamstress who can make it fit perfectly."

"Sounds great! My pre-pregnancy size was a two, so a four should be safe, in case I don't lose the baby weight by June."

Angelina noticed for the first time the dark smudges Savannah had tried to conceal under her eyes. She'd been so preoccupied with picking out her wedding dress that she hadn't seen them sooner. She gave Savannah a quick hug, not explaining why, and Savannah hugged her back in equal silence.

They chose a one-shoulder version of the same design for Karla and strapless gowns for the bridesmaids. Angelina imagined how beautiful they'd all look at the church and reception.

Her big day was becoming more real by the moment.

Chapter Three

Angelina plopped down on the bed in one of Karla's guest rooms. Despite it being well after midnight, she was still keyed up. What a wonderful experience this had turned out to be. She'd found her dress, and while the April delivery date made her a tad nervous, Amanda didn't think the dress would require anything but minor alterations.

Sharing this momentous day with Mama and several members of her bridal party—not to mention having Megan preserving the memories with her camera—topped it all off. She couldn't wait to show Cassie and Pippa photos of the gown. Pippa was holding down the fort at the restaurant until tomorrow afternoon, while Cassie and Luke were in Peru after finding out her father had been hospitalized last week. Marc said Luke told him Mr. López was home recuperating now, but they'd chosen to stay a while longer so Cassie could take him to Machu Picchu during the warm-weather season down there.

Her phone's text alert went off, startling her. Seeing Marc's name on the screen made her heart swell. He was doing a twenty-four-hour ride time at the Aspen Corners Fire Department, where Rafe and Tony worked, as part of his clinicals for EMT certification. She'd missed talking to him today but didn't want to interfere.

MARC: U up?

ANGELINA: Wide awake.

MARC: Wearing ur new dress?

ANGELINA: Haha. Don't have it this fast. Ordered, tho.

MARC: Can't wait to see u in it.

ANGELINA: Not until our wedding day. You'll luv it.

MARC: I'd love u in any dress. Or nothing at all.

Just as she'd been thinking earlier today. The three dots indicated he was texting something more, so she waited and then read:

MARC: What are u wearing?

Angelina grinned. Was he in the mood to sext tonight? She wouldn't be home from Karla's until late tomorrow morning but wouldn't be alone with Marc until after the restaurant closed. Even though she'd only missed one full day at work, her staff was still relatively new and not able to handle every situation that might come their way yet, so she'd go straight to the restaurant after dropping off Mama.

Remembering that he'd asked her a question, she refocused.

ANGELINA: Tank top & panties.

MARC: No Mama?

He knew she'd be wearing much more if sharing a bedroom with Mama. Maybe he wanted to make sure the coast was clear before they got into this any deeper.

ANGELINA: Has her own room. Remember how enormous this house is? Will come in handy when the triplets want separate rooms.

The house had been too massive for bachelor Marc but was perfect for Adam and Karla's growing family. However, size probably wasn't the real issue. Marc and Angelina were building a beautiful log house nearly the same size near the reservoir, halfway between Aspen Corners and Breckenridge. Living on the side of a mountain much better suited them than a house in the city.

MARC: Which room are u in?

ANGELINA: 1st on the left.

MARC: Ah. Can picture u better now.

ANGELINA: Where should I picture u?

MARC: Outside the station. Snuck out while they're sleeping.

Angelina hoped Marc and the guys would have a slow night and no one would need their services. But she appreciated that he'd take time to text her.

MARC: Play with ur nipples.

His command sent a zing to her clit and a smile to her face. He hadn't told her to remove the top yet, so she pinched and pulled at them one at a time through her tank with one hand while holding the phone with the other. She almost held her breath while waiting for his next text.

MARC: Have u made my nipples hard, just the way I would if I were there?

ANGELINA: Yes, Sir.

His sitting outside the station in plain view would make this illicit conversation even hotter for him. Would she get him so hot he'd have to find a more secluded spot to touch himself? Could she make him come? Luckily, he couldn't see the mischief in her eyes, or she wouldn't be sitting comfortably for days. But she planned to pursue this for all she was worth.

ANGELINA: Yes, Sir. Like bullets.

MARC: I need to see. Lift ur top, pet. Send a pic.

Without hesitation, she snapped two photos and first sent a

"not safe for work" warning. Even though he was a student and not an employee, he wouldn't want to jeopardize his reputation if caught in the act. Good thing everyone else was asleep at the moment.

Angelina giggled as she put in a few returns so that her semi-nude pics wouldn't show up on his preview screen and then attached the two shots—one looking down at both of her girls and the other a closeup of her hardest nipple. She clicked send and smiled at his almost immediate response.

MARC: Fuck, woman. Don't worry. I don't share my gorgeous girl with anyone.

He added a fire emoji at the end of the text. Empowered and horny as hell, Angelina responded.

ANGELINA: I miss you, Sir, and what u did to me last night.

His next emojis were of a waving hand and a peach. Clearly, he remembered, too.

ANGELINA: I wish you were spanking my ass right now.

MARC: Topping? Behave. I can deprive u of what u crave as ur punishment.

Her clit throbbed, despite his warning. It was a bad habit she didn't think he really wanted her to break. Marc loved his little brat.

ANGELINA: Sorry, Sir.

But not *sorry.*

Next she texted him two rain emojis and the words:

ANGELINA: I'm wet, Sir.

The screen changed to an incoming call as her phone vibrated.

Marc. She accepted the call. "Hello, sweetheart." Her voice sounded husky.

Without preamble, he said in a low voice, "Put the phone on its stand and switch to speaker." She followed his commands, staying in submissive role without stopping to chitchat.

Dio, *I miss him.*

Apparently, he wanted her hands free and would be giving her verbal commands now. She needed some relief after the stress-filled moments earlier in the day when she wasn't sure she'd ever find a dress she and Mama could agree on.

Angelina set the phone on speaker and placed it in the holder on the nightstand before stretching out on the bed.

"Ready, Sir."

"Slip your hand inside your panties from the waistband. Get your finger wet in my pussy and circle your clit slowly eight times."

She couldn't believe how drenched she was already, just from a few suggestive texts. Already close to coming, she rubbed her clit slowly, barely touching the excited bundle of nerves. She wanted to last a while.

"I'm so wet. Only for you, Sir."

"Slowly insert a finger into my pussy."

She moved her finger lower along her slit again, knowing that this wouldn't feel nearly as good as touching her clit. Her finger slid inside easily.

"Feel full yet?"

"Not as full as I am with your penis inside me."

"Sounds like you need more."

"Oh, yes, Sir! I do! My finger is a sorry substitute for you."

"Slide three fingers into my pussy." His voice sounded huskier. "But don't move until my command."

Three fingers were closer to what his cock felt like, but still a sorry imitation because she couldn't angle them in the way his penis would feel.

"Pull out and ram them inside you three times."

Despite the awkward angle, the jarring of her clit while attempting this command made her clit zing.

"Now, slowly stroke your clit with your thumb until you're at the edge of coming, but you do NOT have permission to come."

She groaned. He laughed. She treated him to a few seconds of heavy breathing then let out a moan.

"Fuck, woman. You're killing me."

Angelina smiled. "Please, Sir. Let me come."

"Topping again, pet?"

"Sorry, Sir." *Not sorry.*

"I want you to masturbate to this scenario. You're lying over my lap, ass bare and red hot from the blistering you just received for being such a brat."

Oh, yes! Obviously, he wasn't really upset with her, because if he was, he'd know the promise of a spanking would *not* be a deterrent for her bad behavior.

She imagined the feel of his firm hand on her butt and stroked faster until she was at the edge and had to slow down before she came without permission.

"I'm there, Sir."

"Do not come. I want you to picture me inserting a butt plug first."

Mio Dio, she wasn't going to last if he kept suggesting doing all the things she wished he was doing to her. If Mama wasn't traveling with her, she'd hop in the SUV and drive home tonight to be naked and waiting for him after he came home in the morning.

"Please, Sir! You know I'm not going to last much longer if you torture me like that!"

Marc's diabolical laugh told her he would show her no mercy. Maybe he *was* disciplining her for topping him earlier.

"Plug's almost in. Your ass is fucking tight."

She groaned, slowly stroking her clit as she imagined the sensation. "I wish I'd brought my vibe with me for the full effect."

"There you go again. I think you have an active enough imagination not to need the actual stimulation. Bring yourself to the edge again while I'm smacking your ass now that the plug's all the way in."

He made a slapping sound, then again, each one reverberating against the plug and into her pussy. Her thumb circled her clit slowly to keep from coming, but she was so close she was afraid to go too far and blow the incredible orgasm he had in store for her.

"Sir, pleeeeease show some mercy for your naughty brat! I can't hold out much longer!"

"Yes, you can."

Bastardo!

"I heard that."

She hadn't spoken out loud, had she?

"Even if you only thought it."

She smiled. Yes, he did know her well.

"All right. When I give the command for you to come, I want to hear you all the way from Denver." She thought about the others sleeping along this hallway. Turning toward the windows, she moved the phone—still on speaker—against her mouth and placed a pillow over her head to muffle some of the sound.

"What about the others at the station?"

"Sleeping still." She doubted he'd have the volume turned up too loudly, especially since he'd told her earlier that Tony would be on duty for his ride-time shift. But the thought of being overheard by someone other than her brother only added to her excitement.

Marc made another slapping sound as if striking his hand against his bare forearm. She flinched as if he'd struck her butt and regained her focus.

"Please, Sir. I need this. Now!"

"Yes, you do. And you'll get it—when *I'm* ready. Don't forget who's in charge of your orgasms."

She hoped her groan came through as loud and clear as his laughter did.

"I'm ramming my fingers inside you, hard and fast. So hot. So wet for me."

"Y-y-y-esss! I am!"

"Now I'm reaching around with my other hand and pressing against the butt plug, wiggling it."

Dio, she wasn't going to last another minute if he kept this up.

Slap.

Slap.

Slap.

The sound of his spanking her against the plug jolted through her as if she could actually feel his fingers hitting against it. Her thumb bumped against her clit with each smack. The pressure became unbearable, bordering on pain. *Don't come. Do. Not. Come.*

"Come for me, *amore*. Loudly."

The explosive orgasm ripped through her. "Marc! Oh *Dio*, Marc! Yes!" It felt like it went on for minutes, although it was probably mere seconds.

"I can't hear you, pet."

"Yessss!" she screamed, sure everyone in the house could hear her but no longer caring. "I'm coming so hard for you, Sir!"

Slap.

Slap.

After the orgasm crested, she continued to lightly stroke her clit until it became too sensitive to touch.

"*Gesù*, woman. I didn't think this through. I'm going to have blue balls until I see you."

She gasped for air until she could speak coherently. "You...started it."

"Is someone looking to be disciplined tomorrow instead of enjoying something more along the lines of double penetration?"

"*Sir*, I mean." Maybe she should try to return the favor. "May I kneel in front of you and take that big, hard cock into my mouth, Sir?"

His guttural expletive made her smile. To know she had that kind of effect on him from eighty miles away made her feel like a super hero. "If I were Wonder Woman, I'd be there to give you relief in the blink of an eye."

"Great. Now you have me picturing you in a breastplate with your golden Lasso of Truth wrapped around my waist as you reel me in. You're killing me, pet."

"But what a way to go!" Her mind already thought ahead to the next costume night at the club this fall. She grabbed a couple tissues from the nightstand to clean off her fingers and picked up the phone again. "Please? May I give you a virtual blow job, Sir?"

"I appreciate the offer, but I'd rather wait until I can get your luscious lips around my cock in person."

She'd expected no less. Marc took his EMT training seriously and wouldn't compromise his reputation, considering this was the station he hoped to be hired by after earning his certification.

"If you insist, Sir. But I promise to do all kinds of lecherous things to you tomorrow night after I get home."

"Fuck. I can't wait *that* long. Maybe I can spirit you away from the restaurant before the dinner crowd for a quickie in your office."

The thought of a staff member discovering them in a compromising position both horrified and excited her. However, facing them again afterward reminded her that her own career and professionalism were equally important. "How about the apartment upstairs from the restaurant? I've kept it vacant for when a staff member needs a place to crash in bad weather or whenever. I haven't gotten a bed in there yet. Just the sofa. However, the granite countertop in the kitchen should meet our needs." They often played in their own kitchen.

"I wish I could drive all the way to Adam's house as soon as I'm done in the morning, but I'd probably pass you and your mama on I-70. So tomorrow afternoon it must be."

She relaxed against the pillows feeling extremely mellow and oh so loved. "Thank you for tonight, Sir. I needed some relief like you can't imagine."

"Dress shopping was that rough, huh?"

"Brutal—but when I found the right one, it made it all worthwhile. I can't wait for you to see it."

"Neither can I, *cara*. Partly because that means all this wedding planning shit will be over, and we can get on to the fun stuff—like the wedding night and honeymoon."

"Most definitely!" Not that she wanted them to breeze through one of the most important days of their shared life. "Oh, I almost forgot. Tomorrow, after the lunch crowd is gone, we have another planning thing to get done, but I think you'll like this one."

He groaned. "What do we have to do?"

"We have an appointment with the baker to sample wedding cakes."

"Definitely count me in for that."

"The baker is right in Breckenridge, so we won't lose too much time from our other plans."

"I intend to sample cakes by licking frosting off your tits."

The thought of his tongue licking the icing from her nipples had her clit throbbing again. How did he do that? "Now you have *me* fantasizing about that, too. Maybe he'll let us take a few slices back to the apartment to experiment with afterward."

"Our afternoon rendezvous is sounding better by the minute." He sighed. "But you have a long drive ahead of you, so get some sleep. I'll just sit here picturing you covered in wedding cake and frosting the rest of the night. Love you, baby."

"You get some sleep, too, Marc." She worried about how little he slept and the detrimental effects sleep deprivation had on people working in emergency services. "I promise you'll need your strength."

She'd better end this conversation. Already she needed to come again but wouldn't be greedy or selfish. "Good night, sweetheart. I'll text you when I'm caught up with prep, supply ordering, and bill paying at the restaurant. Then we'll taste cakes before you properly fuck me."

His hearty laugh, followed by "before *and* after," made her wonder if she'd be able to take that much time away after being gone for almost two days already. While she missed him so much, she didn't want to fall further behind at work.

"Just joking. After will have to suffice, but I'll make sure you're properly fucked. Oh, pack one of your medium-sized vibes with a wide base on it."

Her clit zinged. "Yes, Sir," she said, already getting hot for the double-penetration scene he planned. Tomorrow couldn't arrive fast enough.

Chapter Four

"**D**efinitely the amaretto." Marc nibbled the last piece of the almond-flavored cake he'd smeared on her breasts fifteen minutes ago before licking the icing off her nipple and drawing that hard peak into his mouth to suck.

"Oh yes! Definitely the amaretto!" she screamed, breathless.

He'd never known wedding cake could be so delectable. She pushed her chest up to relieve the force of his tongue while at the same time wrapping her legs around his waist as if to lock him in.

"I haven't been served up as dessert in a long time, but I've always loved the way you play with your food—and me."

Lifting his head, he stared into her chocolate-brown eyes. "Every time I look at you, I think dessert, *cara*."

So delectable, Angelina lay stretched out on her back on the granite countertop of the kitchen island in the apartment above her restaurant. He'd known it would be the amaretto cake as soon as he took a bite at the baker's an hour ago, but having fantasized about eating cake off Angelina's body since last night, hours after the hot-as-fuck sexting and phone sex they'd enjoyed, he had no intention of rushing to judgment.

Merda! Reality beat the hell out of his imagination.

He took her swollen nipple between his teeth and tugged higher than she could try to evade.

"Oh!" She smiled. "Careful what you bite into there, sailor."

Marc chomped down a little harder on her nipple to remind her who was in charge, and she gasped again. Her hands gripped the edges of the counter, just where he'd told her to keep them.

Knowing he'd only succeed at keeping her mind off work another half hour or so, he ordered, "Plant your feet wide for me."   .

Angelina tented her knees, placing her feet at the edges of the countertop as wide as they could go without slipping off. With her glistening pussy wet and ready, he couldn't resist playing a little while longer.

Bending down, he swirled his tongue over her clit in slow motion. He'd make her beg for his cock before he'd give it to her. Marc plunged a finger into her tight, wet hole. Damn. Maybe he wouldn't be able to hold out long enough for her to beg. It had been two days since they'd made love. Last night's phone call had left him needing to bury himself into her in the worst way.

When he drove two fingers inside her and sped up the movement of his tongue, she hissed. "I need you inside me, Marc."

A start, but not nearly the level of need he wanted from her. "Did you pack what I asked you to when you stopped by the house this morning?"

"Yes, Sir. It's in my purse."

He wished he'd thought to bring his toy bag with his collection of butt plugs, but time was limited. He couldn't go home and retrieve it before she needed to return to the restaurant.

Imagining where he planned to put the vibe made Marc harder. They'd both been too damned busy to fit each other in lately between coursework, studying, the restaurant, and wedding preparations. They needed this interlude together.

He pulled away, and she groaned. "Tell me what you want, *cara.*"

"I want...I want your hard cock ramming in and out of me and a vibrator up my ass."

Fuck, woman. He pulled his fingers out of her pussy and crossed to the living room to find her purse where she'd dropped it when he'd pushed her against the wall for a long, hard kiss seconds after they'd closed the door.

He found the vibe in the side compartment inside a zippered plastic bag and, beside it, a small tube of lubricant. Her pussy never had a problem being wet enough for him, so clearly she'd anticipated anal, too. *That's my girl.* They always seemed to be on the same wavelength.

The long, slim vibe wasn't nearly as thick as his cock, but he hadn't entered her ass in a while, so he'd have to prepare her for him before resuming that activity. The vibe would get to have a majority of the fun today, but he wasn't complaining.

When he returned to the island, Angelina's eyes remained closed. Her voluptuous, sexy body lay ready for him to continue to feast on. "What are you fantasizing about?"

"Double penetration."

His cock throbbed at her earthy response, and he released it from his pants to stroke himself at the image she conjured up. He didn't care if she pictured another man with him in her fantasy. That might be hot to some, but he didn't intend to share this woman with anyone else ever again. "That can be arranged."

Her smile turned sultry at the promise he left hanging.

"Scoot to the edge of the counter and put your legs over my shoulders."

She moved into position until her ass cheeks spilled over the edge, and he lifted her legs. He coated the vibe in lubricant and bent down to flick his tongue against her clit to heighten her senses.

After a few minutes of listening to her panting, he pressed the vibe to the opening of her asshole, without turning it on or entering her. He'd wait until she needed more stimulation, but right now, the grip of her hands and the mewling sounds coming from her told him she was building up to one helluva climax already.

Standing again, he pressed his cock against her pussy, alternately dipping his cock inside to lubricate it while pushing the vibe against her back door.

"Marc! You're killing me! I need to come, now!"

"Pet, might I remind you who's calling the shots?"

She groaned, her eyes squeezing shut. He continued to go in a little farther, each stroke of his cock feeling her pussy welcoming him home. Sweat broke out on her forehead, and she nibbled at her lower lip as if biting back further demands. Her drenched pussy told him she was ready for the entire length of him. For now, he set the vibe on the baggie beside her hip and plowed his cock fully into her in one swift motion.

"Yes! *Mio Dio!*"

Pumping fast and hard for a few minutes until he nearly exploded inside her, he savored the way she clamped her pussy muscles around him. *"Gesù, amore!"* He wasn't going to be able to hold out much longer but wasn't ready to let go just yet. He wanted her to explode more powerfully than she had in a long time. Definitely harder than last night when he wasn't even physically with her.

He picked up the vibrator again, flicked the switch on its lowest setting, and pressed it against her puckered star.

"Ack! Yes! Oh! Permission to come, Sir?"

"Not yet." He pushed the vibe harder against her sphincter then pulled back as he thrust his cock inside her and alternated between the two. Each time he withdrew from her pussy, she gripped his cock harder. His balls became painful as he rammed himself home again. This time, he stayed put and pushed the vibe inside her a few inches, feeling the vibrations against his cock.

He couldn't hold out any longer. "Come with me, *amore.*"

"I'm coming!"

Her pussy squeezed him like a vise as his cock pulsated with his ejaculate. "Right. There. With you."

"Marc! Give it to me! Give it all to me!"

He thrust harder, faster as his cum spurted inside her hot pussy.

"Yes! Like that! Oh, Marc!" She rutted against his pelvis to milk every ounce of her own orgasm from him. Seeing her in the throes of passion only made his own that much hotter.

When his cock stopped twitching, he placed the vibe in the baggie for cleaning later and pulled out of her. His cum spilled out of her. They hadn't been very careful today, but he didn't care if babies came earlier than they'd planned. He wanted a houseful of little D'Alessios.

"That was...amazing," she said when she opened her eyes to smile up at him.

"No, you're the amazing one." He wiped her off with paper towels and helped her up. "I can picture us like this seventy years from now, and I'll be just as hot for you then as I am now."

Angelina laughed. "I'm not sure how agile I'll be at ninety-six, but you know I'll always be hot for your hundred-and-five-year-old bod," she said, slapping him on the ass before enfolding him in an embrace and a kiss. "Thanks for the afternoon delight. I'm going to be thinking about you until I close tonight."

"You know I'm going to be in the same headspace while waiting for you to get home. Maybe someday we'll be independently wealthy and won't have to worry about making a living."

She shook her head, smiling. "That's just the orgasm talking, Marc. Your work as an EMT is a calling just as strongly felt as one to the priesthood. That's how my brothers and Papa looked at their vocations, too. No amount of money will change that."

"True."

"We're both always going to be passionate about our work, just maybe not *as* passionate as we are about sex sometimes. We have to get more creative about carving out some time for ourselves."

"Well, today shows me there's no lacking in our taking initiative in that department."

None, indeed.

Chapter Five

"This is going to be much more fun than the wedding shower Mama gave us in April," Angelina said as they walked in the back door to the Masters at Arms Club.

"And by the time we're done, my toy bag will be stuffed with all kinds of new things to torment you with, I'm sure."

Angelina's first thought was whether Luke would be bringing some new wooden torture device tonight. Would he and Cassie even be attending? Cassie definitely wasn't in the lifestyle. Not that he wouldn't have sent a new toy as a companion to the paddle he'd given them two Christmases ago. That one had MINE carved out of it and left the word emblazoned on her ass with every blow. *Not* her favorite implement, although Marc seemed to enjoy the hell out of it.

In the great room, everyone she expected to see had already arrived—the Montagues, Orlandos, Wilsons, Mistress Grant, and, yes, even the Dentons. How Luke had talked Cassie into coming inside the BDSM club was beyond her, but Cassie was smiling and talking to Savannah.

They spent the first half hour nibbling on appetizers and sipping soft drinks, which implied there might be some playing going on later. The social time had been followed by bridal shower games with kinky prizes for the winners, including nipple clamps, paddles, floggers, and a Wartenberg wheel.

When Cassie won one of their earlier games, she'd looked over the items on the prize table with wide, curious eyes before picking up the wheel saying, "I'll take this pretty pattern-tracing wheel."

"Oh, honey," Karla said to her, "we need to talk."

"What? You people have come up with perverted uses for this, too?" Cassie asked, holding it up, and the room was filled with good-natured laughter. Cassie shook her head but smiled. It was amazing how far she'd come out of her reclusive shell since she met and married Luke. Angelina surmised that some "vanilla" sensation play might be in her near future with that wheel. She shivered thinking about how delicious the spikes had felt against her own skin, especially her breasts, that first time Marc had played with Nonna's actual tracing wheel in her bedroom.

When all the prizes on the table had been claimed, Karla instructed Ryder and Luke to position two chairs back to back in the center of the circle, and Adam indicated that Angelina and Marc each be seated in one.

"Vanilla people play this next game with shoes. But we aren't vanilla. Well, most of us aren't."

Everyone laughed again, and Cassie blushed before saying, "Not entirely vanilla anymore. I have learned a few things I've enjoyed from Luke."

"Oh-ho!" came the shouts of a few of the men, several clapping Luke on the back.

"Don't y'all be teasing my darlin' now," he said.

Adam cleared his throat to gain their attention again. "Now I'm going to ask some questions, and all you have to do, Marc and Angelina, is hold up a paddle if your response is Marc or a wooden spoon if the answer is Angelina."

Karla handed both a spoon. Angelina received the pink fuzzy paddle Marc had first used on her early in their relationship. Marc was given the MINE paddle Luke had made as a Christmas gift for them.

"Karla's going to keep track of how many times you two agree with each other—and how often you don't." Adam paused, and

Angelina wondered if there was a prize awarded if the agreements outnumbered the wrong guesses, but he didn't say more.

"Okay, let's get started. First question: Who's messier?"

That was easy. She lifted the spoon. Marc's Navy training hadn't worn off all these years later. Everyone clapped, so apparently they'd agreed with one another. No problem there.

"Next, who's the most stubborn?"

Oh boy. She'd have to give that one a little more thought. "Angelina?" Adam asked. Apparently, Marc had a response. They were both stubborn, so who was worse? She lifted the paddle, but everyone groaned. So Marc thought *she* was more stubborn, did he?

"Next question. If I lined up all of Marc's floggers in no particular order, who would rearrange them in order of size and/or color?"

That was another easy one. Marc had asked her to do that before, so she lifted the paddle again. Cheers. Another time they were in agreement.

"Who takes longer showers?"

Up went her spoon, and everyone clapped, so he must have agreed. Again, easy answer due to his Navy training. Marc stuck to his two-minute showers—unless they were in there together and they *both* stayed the same amount of time.

Stubborn, indeed. Overall, though, they were doing fairly well and had only disagreed on one. Maybe they would get a reward rather than a punishment. Around here, though, it was sometimes hard to tell the difference.

"If there was one chocolate left in the bowl," Adam began, "who would be more likely to give it to the other?"

Angelina was a pleaser, so she lifted the spoon.

"Awww, it's so sweet you two would give it to each other," Cassie said.

"Master Adam," Karla added, "I'd probably keep it and not tell you about it."

Everyone laughed.

"Good to know," he said.

"I love watching Angelina enjoy chocolate," Marc said, "so I'd receive much more pleasure watching her eat it than keeping it myself."

"I'd better stock up on Hershey's kisses for the wedding night," she said.

More laughter. Everyone seemed to be having fun with the game, even if they weren't in the hot seats.

"Let's open it up for others to ask questions," Adam said. "Anyone?"

"Who made the first move?" Damián asked.

She raised the spoon indicating she'd been first. Then she had second thoughts. "Wait! I guess that depends on if you mean here at the club or when we met a month later at daVinci's."

"No explanations allowed," Adam declared. "Too late anyway. Marc says it was him, so no score there. Next question?"

"Who can go the longest without having an orgasm during play?" Grant asked.

Two paddles were raised. "Poor Marc had blue balls when we first started scening together," Angelina said.

"Who knew it was love first?" Savannah asked quietly.

"I'm sure we will agree on this one," Marc said as both he and Angelina raised a spoon. "She taught me the meaning of love."

"That is so sweet," said Cassie. "Okay, my question is who would most likely give in first in a disagreement?" Both agreed it would be Angelina.

"I aim to please!" she explained with a shrug.

"Which one can get the other off quicker?" Luke asked. Another difference of opinion, with each saying it was the other.

"On the flip side, who is more likely to withhold sex as punishment?" Ryder asked.

Once again, they hadn't agreed. Angelina was certain she'd be the guilty party, but Marc saw it differently.

"You two seem to be disagreeing more lately," Adam pointed out. "I guess my questions were cream puffs, but there's time for one more. Megan, you've been awfully quiet. Do you have a question?"

"Who wishes you'd decided to elope at this point?" Megan asked. She and Ryder had chosen that path themselves, and Angelina sometimes fantasized about what it would have been like if she and Marc had done so, too.

Torn, Angelina knew she had to be honest, so she raised both the paddle *and* the spoon. Laughter and a shouted "Angelina!" chorus broke out. She couldn't resist turning to see that Marc had raised only the paddle.

He also turned to face her to see what the commotion was about and grinned. "You should have listened to me last year, *amore*, when I first proposed the idea."

She shrugged. "Too late now."

"Sorry," Adam said, "but technically, you didn't completely agree on that one, so that's another one in the disagreed column. Before you drift any farther apart, maybe we need to call a halt to further questioning now," Adam said. "Kitten, what's our score?"

"Well, we have a tie—six in each column."

"Interesting," he said. "Then it looks like we'll have to reward—or punish, as the case may be—both of them."

"Who are you talking about punishing?" Marc asked. "That was just a silly game."

"Don't worry, Doc," Adam assured him with a chuckle. "We aren't talking about anything remotely like the interrogation scene. Just a few whacks with one of those paddles—one for each of the six times you couldn't agree."

"How's that a punishment for Angelina?" Marc argued. "She loves being spanked."

Angelina had to admit her heartbeat ramped up at the thought of a good, hard spanking tonight. *Poor Marc.* He hated being paddled, although she doubted his friends would take this too far.

"You're absolutely right. That's why Angelina is going to be the one wielding the paddle."

Had she heard Adam correctly?

"Come again?" Marc asked.

Apparently so. No way was she interested in topping her man again. "I don't think—"

"Nor should you," Adam said in his Dom voice, brooking no further discussion.

Now Angelina could see how this would be a punishment for her as well. She waited to see how this would develop as a scene. "Angelina, choose the position you want him in."

Could she do this? Marc hadn't responded well when she'd tried paddling him before. The women from his past had done a number on him, and she didn't want to stir up those emotions in him again.

"Let's get this over with, pet."

He wanted to go through with it? She glanced around the room, noticing the loveseat just to the right of the stage. No, she wouldn't do anything that would mimic the paddling episodes from his past. Then she saw the center post where he'd restrained and flogged her the first time they played together here. She pointed to the post, "I'd like him restrained there with his hands above his head."

Adam dug a pair of leather wrist cuffs from his toy bag and tossed them to her. She caught them deftly before Adam said, "That's your job, Mistress Angelina."

He hadn't called her Mistress *A*, which led her to believe Marc had never revealed that she'd topped him once before. She liked that Adam didn't know everything about their bedroom relationship and smiled as she closed the gap between her and Marc.

"Sir, it pains me to have to do this, but do you agree to this short-term power reversal?"

He pressed his lips together, flattening them out as he glanced at Adam. Would Marc go through with it?

"I'm not sure I have a choice."

Oh, Marc. Her heart ached for him. "You always have a choice if I'm in charge," she assured him.

His gaze zeroed in on her, and his mouth relaxed a little. "I taught you well."

Her heart grew warm at his acknowledgement and his apparent acquiescence. "Indeed, you did." She squared her shoulders and held up the first cuff between them. "If you're ready, left wrist, please."

Soon she had both of his wrists cuffed and clipped together and led him to the post where she asked Adam to assist her in lifting Marc's hands high enough over his head.

"Up on those toes, boy," she ordered. In his leathers, she couldn't really ask him to spread his legs as wide as he'd had her do that first time he'd chained her to this same post.

Adam pulled Marc's wrists higher until he was indeed on tiptoe. Then he stepped aside. "Those have panic snaps, Marc, to lower your anxiety level. But I'd better hear you safeword before you bail on the scene." Adam turned to Angelina. "He's all yours, Mistress."

Chapter Six

F uck Adam, anyway, for putting him in this position. He knew Marc had an aversion to paddles, restraints, and to relinquishing control. What was the point in this ridiculous game anyway? Make him look like a fool in front of his bride-to-be?

Angelina closed the gap and whispered in Marc's ear, "What are your safewords, boy?"

He could tell she was getting into this mistress role again. Sure, the last time had some moments Marc still fantasized about recreating—not that he'd ever asked her to do so—but he'd also had a freak-out during that session he didn't want to repeat in front of his friends or Angelina.

"Red." He wasn't in the mood to come up with a playful word or some kind of food like cannoli. But he'd heed Adam's warning. "Yellow to slow down."

Marc stared at the quick-release snap above him, his safeword on the tip of his tongue while his thumb and forefinger hovered over the mechanism. He could put an end to this in an instant.

She tapped the paddle against the backs of his thighs a few times. "Do you trust me?"

Marc tested his bonds, clenching and unclenching his hands as he tried to prepare himself mentally to be paddled. Sweat broke out on his forehead. Wanting to wipe the telltale sign of nervousness away, he leaned his head against his bicep and gave it a slight turn. Being left vulnerable was not a pleasant feeling or one he wanted to indulge in, especially around Angelina. He was supposed to be the strong one.

Had she been in on this setup from the beginning? If so, she was a damned good actress, because she seemed as surprised as he when Adam proposed this consequence for their not agreeing on more of their responses in that asinine game.

Deep down, though, Marc knew this was all Adam's doing and that he and Angelina were Adam's pawns. Refusing to make eye contact with anyone, Marc dropped his head and hunched closer to the post. *Escape. Hide.* Realizing what he was doing, he pulled away again and placed his focus on the wood grain of the post.

"I asked you a question, S—Marc," Angelina said. Her uncertainty tore at him. *Gesù*, would he ever be able to convince her how much he trusted her? Was this his chance to convey that through actions instead of words?

In a flash, it became crystal clear what Adam was up to. Marc was about to say *I do* to this woman for the rest of his life, and Adam wanted to make sure Marc was indeed ready to forever surrender his heart—and his trust—to her.

Bastardo. But Adam was right, as usual. He needed this.

Marc took a deep breath and released it. "Yes, Mistress, I trust you." As if a weight had been lifted off him, an awareness came over him telling Marc he truly did. "I trust you with my life, *amore.*" He relaxed completely, becoming one with the post and preparing himself for the paddle.

Angelina delivered the first half-hearted blow to his left ass cheek. He couldn't resist taunting her now that he was getting into the spirit of the game. "I think you can do better than that, Mistress."

"Topping from the bottom, boy? Remember your place." Angelina giggled, probably amused that his brat was disciplining her own brat at the moment. All the same, the next blow hit harder on the same spot, followed by an even harder one on the right cheek. Incredibly, he didn't trigger or find himself lost in the past. In fact, as Angelina rained a few more blows onto his ass, his cock started to grow hard.

Might be a little embarrassing when she released him from this post, but knowing that he'd passed the test and was actually enjoying a paddling at the hands of his woman left him too elated to care.

When the paddling stopped, Angelina raked her fingernails down his ass cheeks through the leathers before pressing her body against his. "How is my boy feeling?" she whispered.

"Like he wants to take you into one of the theme rooms and fuck you blind."

Her hips jerked involuntarily against him. "I think that can be arranged."

"What about the party?"

"Everyone's left us alone."

Seriously? "Are you kidding me?"

"No, not kidding." She laughed as she moved to his side. "You can extricate yourself now, since I can't reach that high."

He released the panic snap and lowered his hands for her to unbuckle each cuff. Once freed, he turned around and scanned the great room. Sure enough, they were alone. For how long? He'd thank Adam later for sparing him any humiliation in case he had bailed on the scene. Adam had already achieved his goal—getting Marc to see how deeply he trusted Angelina. She was the first woman he'd trusted outside his mother and sister.

Without warning, he bent and picked her up, carrying her down the hallway to the impact room, their favorite. In the hallway, he heard laughter coming from the kitchen, where apparently the party had been moved without them. Fine by him.

Inside theme room eight, he eyed the Saint Andrew's cross. Angelina had long ago faced her demons from the beating she'd received in this room from that asshole Allen. But he wanted to deliver a flogging she'd never forget, so that's where they would begin. He spied his toy bag in the corner.

Thank you, Adam. He must have moved it here while Marc was tied up, so to speak. Adam had taken care of him yet again.

"Strip for me."

Angelina looked him in the eye momentarily then dropped her gaze to the floor as she slowly removed her blouse. He'd seamlessly taken back control. While she did get into playing the dominant in short runs, ultimately she was a submissive. *His* submissive.

She wore a bustier much like the one she'd worn the first time he'd flogged her. He didn't let her keep it on this time. He wanted to see those gorgeous tits in all their glory.

And Angelina never disappointed. Her nipples were hard as pebbles by the time she slipped the lacy garment off. He wasted no time moving closer and taking one nipple between his teeth and tugging while pinching the other. She gasped, pushing against his mouth for more. He suckled, drawing the rigid peak into his mouth as he pressed his tongue against the bottom of her nipple to suck harder. Her hands wrapped around his head, holding him there, but he pulled away.

"Finish stripping for me, *amore*."

She quickly shed the skirt and panties and stood naked before him. His cock jerked against his leathers.

"Now, I think perhaps it's time for you to feel the squeeze of my cuffs."

She held out her arms, eager to continue. Normally, he'd want to make her wait, but he had no patience tonight. She'd stirred a fire in him he wanted quenched—soon. He didn't intend to have blue balls tonight.

After securing her spread-eagle facing the Saint Andrew's cross with ankle and wrist cuffs, he removed a pair of long floggers from his bag and began warming up. Every now and then, the tips would strike her back or ass and she'd clench her hands, but he didn't begin flogging her immediately. He moved next to her, pressing his cock against her to show her how she affected him.

She moaned, a delicious sound. When he reached in front of her and between her legs, he found her wet and ready for him. With a groan, he pulled away. He at least needed to reward her with a flogging for what she'd helped him realize tonight.

Parting her hair to bare her back to him, he placed the thick locks over each shoulder to rest on her breasts. Taking up his position slightly farther than a yard away, he started the floggers in motion in Florentine style, alternating hands and developing his rhythm. He started on her shoulders and upper back then skipped over the kidney area before speeding up as the falls rained down on her ass and thighs.

She hissed, clenching her hands again. He kept her on edge and guessing where and when the next set of blows would fall. Her ass and shoulders turned red as he continued relentlessly for the next fifteen minutes.

Her head lolled to the side. Had he gotten her to subspace? *Well, hell.* He set the floggers on the spanking bench and moved to Angelina's side.

"*Cara*, can you hear me?"

She moaned, smiling. He lifted her eyelid and found her pupil dilated and unresponsive. He groaned. He'd given her the pleasure she'd deserved, but clearly, they wouldn't be having sex until she came out of it. Angelina didn't orgasm while in subspace. Perhaps no woman could.

Carefully, he removed the ankle cuffs and wrist cuffs, and she slipped into his arms. They'd pick up where they left off later, but she'd earned her reward after her performance as Mistress A. Marc carried her to the harem room, thankful it wasn't occupied, and laid her gently on the raised circular mattress. Shucking his own clothes, he joined her, pulling her against his hard body—every inch of which was still hard—and stroked her arm as he whispered soothing words to her. Anticipation was good for them both.

A smile flitted across her lips as if she'd overheard his thought. He lowered his lips to hers, brushing them lightly, eliciting a sleepy moan from her.

He fully intended to be chasing after this woman the rest of his life and hoped that they'd be blessed with many, many bliss-filled years together.

Chapter Seven

Rehearsal had gone well, and they had all gathered afterward at Rico Donati's bar, daVinci's, for some fabulous food from Bella Montagna provided by his family as the hosts for the meal. Then came time for the traditional speeches. *This ought to be interesting.* Would anyone take this opportunity to roast him?

"Thank you for being here tonight," Papa D'Alessio began, "and I again welcome those who traveled some distance, whether from Denver or from Italy." He paused and turned his attention to Marc. "I will never forget the day you came into my life. You had a delightful way of charming those around you and a smile that could win over anyone."

Hearing Papa, the man who raised him, telling stories of what Marc had been like as a young boy warmed him in unexpected ways. His love for Papa matched how he felt about Adam, although the latter was more like a big brother figure. They would always be the two most important men in his life, having helped shape him into the man he was today.

"Imagine our joy when Marco brought Angelina home to meet us that first time. She won us over in an instant. Mama and I had no doubt that she was the perfect woman for our Marco. Right, Mama?" He gazed at his wife, who nodded, dabbing tears from her eyes.

"Angelina," Papa continued, "you will officially become our second daughter tomorrow, but I raise this glass to you tonight to tell you that you can't be any more loved by us than you already are.

Benvenuta in famiglia!"

He and everyone in the room raised a glass in Angelina's direction. She, too, had tears in her eyes at the warm welcome he'd given her and mouthed the words *thank you* to Papa.

After Papa took his seat again between Sandro and Mama, Marc leaned over to whisper in her ear, "You'll be the best part of the family."

"Oh, Marc, I love your family. Every single one of you. And I'm proud to be a member of it."

Without introduction, Rafe's voice penetrated their private bubble. "I'll never forget the first Sunday Angelina brought Marc home for a family dinner. My little sister hadn't brought many boys home growing up, and I think we all took notice, wondering what was so special about this one." He paused a moment, letting the words hang there, before adding, "...to Angelina."

Rafe's piercing gaze bore into Marc as they were surrounded with laughter. Marc hoped that, by the time he and Angelina celebrated their golden wedding anniversary, he'd have won over all four of his brothers-in-law but especially Rafe. As the family patriarch in the absence of their father, it would be important to Angelina that Rafe accept and approve of him. Marc had screwed up more than a few times and could understand her brother's reluctance when it came to allowing Marc to marry his baby sister.

"But over the past few months and especially tonight," Rafe continued, "I've seen the way he looks at her, the way his family has welcomed her, and the way he made sure earlier that she ate something despite her pre-wedding jitters." The man was quite perceptive; Marc hadn't been aware of his scrutiny. "Marc, we won't have any problems as long as you remain faithful to my baby sister, continue to gaze at Angelina with love, and cherish her as the beautiful gift she is for the rest of your life."

Ignoring the underlying threat in Rafe's words, Marc raised his glass in salute to his future brother-in-law then turned to Angelina, whose eyes brimmed with tears. "It will be my greatest honor and privilege to do so."

*   *   *

Hearing Rafe's acceptance of the man she loved left her speechless and in tears, but even before Rafe had taken his seat, someone across the room tapped a knife against a glass to gain everyone's attention. Angelina turned in the direction of the sound and saw Rico standing with a glass of white wine in hand. What did he have planned? She hadn't expected toasts or speeches from anyone but family and the wedding party tonight.

"Friends and family of Angelina and Marc," he began, "thank you for being here with them to celebrate tonight. Raise your glass in a toast as we prepare to send them off tomorrow on the first day of their journey together as husband and wife."

Everyone raised their glass and drank. Marc shouted, "Thank you for opening your doors for us to have this private party with friends and family, Rico!"

Rico waved away his thanks. "I'm not sure how many of you know this, but this is the very location where Marc found Angelina and their journey together began."

Angelina's face flamed, but she didn't correct Rico's assumption. No way would she admit Marc actually found her being beaten in a private room at his BDSM Club. Only a handful of people present were aware of what happened that night, and she refused to make eye contact with any of them.

Marc leaned over and whispered, "Smile, *amore*, or you're going to give the appearance of being guilty."

She glanced his way and couldn't help but smile at their somewhat private secret. He placed a kiss on her cheek, and she heard a few women say, "Aww."

"Okay, you two, hold off until tomorrow night," Rico said jokingly. "I have something important to say." When he had their attention again, he continued. "Angelina gave me a gift many years ago, something precious to her that caused her pain because it was too closely wrapped up with the memories of her beloved papa."

Papa's Dean Martin vinyl collection had been exactly that—painful to listen to. Mama had insisted that they go to her, but Angelina had difficulty listening to them without tears after Papa passed away. Knowing Rico and his patrons would enjoy them, she'd donated them to him. Lately, however, she'd begun seeking out old Dino tunes on her music app when feeling nostalgic for Papa. Hearing them tonight during their dinner had produced fond memories but no tears.

"My patrons and I have enjoyed them greatly, as you seem to have tonight as well. So I think it's time to return them to you, Angelina. Then you and Marc can dance to those tunes to your heart's content for many, many years in the privacy of your new home."

Angelina's jaw dropped, and her eyes stung. He couldn't possibly know that over the past year she'd begun regretting letting go of the albums, but she never would have asked for them back, either. That Rico was offering them to her touched her so deeply.

She stood and quickly made her way over to Rico, wrapping her arms around him. "Thank you so much. You can't know how much this means to me."

"Oh, I think I do, baby. I saw how you two danced to those songs that first night two years ago. I've been thinking about doing this for a while now, but, well, life got in the way."

Angelina wondered what was going on with her friend. She used to spend so much time at daVinci's before meeting Marc. Maybe she'd try and catch up with him sometime this summer, although she didn't know when that would happen realistically. "You're a good man and a good friend, Rico." She hugged him again, dabbing at her eyes before returning to her seat where Marc waited for her.

Marc squeezed her hand then asked, "How about a preview of tomorrow's dancing?" He stood and helped her to her feet. They walked over to the jukebox. After he made a selection, Marc led her onto the dance floor.

The opening strains of "All I Do is Dream of You" filled the room, and he drew her into his embrace. She smiled at his album choice as she rested her cheek against his chest and closed her eyes.

"You look incredible in that dress, *cara*. The color suits you."

"Mama said it's traditional for an Italian bride to wear green the night before her wedding." Angelina had never heard of that, but while shopping for Mama's dress, she hadn't been able to take her eyes off the cap-sleeved, emerald green, tea-length dress. Mama had insisted on paying for it when she bought her mother-of-the-bride dress.

"Still, as beautiful as you are in it, I wish you were going home with me tonight so I could strip you out of it the minute we walk in the door."

Angelina smiled as the breath caught in her throat. She'd be staying at Mama's with her bridal party so they could begin getting their hair and makeup done early for the two o'clock wedding.

"I'm going to miss you tonight," he said. "But you'll be foremost in my dreams, *amore*."

"And you, mine."

The whimsical "Let's Put Out the Lights (And Go to Sleep)" began to play as other couples joined them on the dance floor. It was one of Papa and Mama's favorites. The song about a couple looking back on many years of marital bliss made her wonder about the years ahead of them. Would their love grow stronger than it was tonight? While Marc hadn't been easy to love at first, Angelina wanted to be nowhere else in this world but in his arms for the rest of her life.

No cute baby we can spank.

"The only cute baby that's getting spanked in our home will be you, *amore*," Marc said. Adam and Karla, dancing nearby, laughed out loud—whether over Marc's words or the line in the song, she wasn't sure.

Her thoughts turned to another aspect of their relationship. While they'd probably never be more than bedroom role players with an occasional dungeon visit for social reasons, she couldn't wait for them to explore their special BDSM room in their new log home. Marc had had a fantastic playroom in the house he'd sold to Adam, but this one was assembled with only the two of them and their favorite activities in mind. It was much more personal to her than the other one.

When the song ended, she started to pull away, but he wouldn't let go. "One more. I'm going to hate not sleeping with you tonight in our bed and want to hold you as long as I can."

"Dream A Little Dream of Me" followed on the album. Movement around them told her the other couples were still dancing, too, so she settled against his chest again and became lost in the music—and Marc. This might be the longest night of her life. She'd become accustomed to his twenty-four-hour shift every third day since becoming an EMT in January. Tonight felt different, though. The evening stirred emotions always lying under the surface, leaving her missing Papa and raw from the loss. She wanted her man to hold and comfort her. But she wouldn't change plans on Mama at this juncture. From tomorrow night until death parted them, she'd have Marc's arms around her whenever he wasn't on duty.

"Thank you for not giving up on me, *amore*."

She pulled away and smiled up at him. "How could I? You captured my heart and wouldn't let go."

He lowered his lips to her upturned ones and kissed her long and deep. Applause erupted around them, and they parted. Angelina's cheeks grew warm, for some odd reason. She'd be kissing him in front of the entire congregation tomorrow. Mama started preparing to head to the house. Knowing their time tonight was coming to an end, she pulled Marc aside for a proper farewell.

"I'm the one who's going to be blue tonight, dreaming more than a little dream of you, Marc."

"Get some sleep, *amore*. We have a big day ahead of us tomorrow."

"You do the same." It would probably be easier for him up there alone on the mountain in their gorgeous new home than it would be in Mama's small house with all her friends, although that was part of the wedding experience, too.

She wanted it all.

* * *

Marc downed the rest of his Birra Moretti and set the bottle on the bar. He and Franco had been talking about his and Angelina's nonna's neighborhood in Marsala giving him more ideas for the day he would take Angelina back to Sicily.

The door to daVinci's opened and closed, but Marc stayed focused on the conversation. The rehearsal dinner had ended an hour ago when the girls left, but some of the guys had decided to hang out a while longer. Marc wasn't looking forward to returning to the house alone tonight. He already missed her.

"We spent a lot of time at the family's church. Nonna insisted on taking us to Mass every single morning of the week at an ungodly hour."

Angelina and Marc weren't overly religious, so he might not have thought about taking her to church, but he made a mental note to go to a Mass with her in her ancestral home parish.

"Be sure you take her on a stroll through Piazza della Loggia. Nonna let us go there on our own."

"What did she like most about it?"

"Well, well, Marco. Drowning your sorrows the night before being saddled with the old ball and chain?"

Fuck. What was she doing here?

54

Chapter Eight

M arc turned around to find Melissa the Bitch, as Angelina referred to her, standing behind him. She'd tried everything she could to come between them last year but had been no match for Angelina. When Melissa had been vanquished to Omaha, they'd thought they'd heard the last of her.

Not wanting Franco or his brothers to overhear the way he intended to speak to Melissa, Marc excused himself. Grabbing her by the elbow, he hauled Melissa into the now-deserted pool room. He didn't want Angelina's brothers to think he disrespected women, but Melissa was in a class of her own—a very low one—and didn't command any respect from him whatsoever.

"What are you doing here?" he demanded. He kept his voice low but didn't curb his vehemence.

She reached up to stroke his cheek and smiled. "Is that any way to greet your former fiancée?"

He brushed her hand away. "*Former* being the operative word." Thank God Angelina had left before Melissa the Bitch had shown up. Nothing and no one would mar their wedding. It was his job to make sure Melissa didn't crash their day tomorrow.

"I've stayed away to give you a chance to miss me, but I was shocked to see the announcement online that you actually intend to marry that...*girl.*"

She said it as if Angelina were less experienced or sophisticated than she or that she would rather call her by some derogatory term, but Marc had no intention of engaging in conversation with Melissa any longer than necessary. The bitch needed to be gone. Tonight.

"Angelina is everything a man could want in his wife and life partner—and I'm the lucky bastard she said *yes* to." He leaned closer, noticing how much make up she wore these days, and the cloying scent of her too-heavy perfume nearly closed up his throat.

"I don't know what you think you're going to gain by showing up here, but you aren't fit to be anywhere near Angelina. Now crawl back under whatever rock you've been hiding under—in Omaha or wherever—and leave us the hell alone."

She laughed as if he'd just shared some special memory from their past or a private joke. Great. The Giardano brothers were going to have his hide, especially Rafe. He still didn't trust Marc as far as he could throw him. He wanted Rafe's trust and acceptance and was trying hard to get him to believe he'd never hurt Angelina again.

Melissa placed her hand on his chest, and Marc took a step back as if it were a claw with sharp talons.

"Melissa, you disgust me. Whether you can accept that or not in your delusional world isn't my problem, but if you show up tomorrow or ever come anywhere near Angelina or me again, you'll be sorry."

"Threats, Marco? How gauche."

The woman had to be mentally unbalanced, but she wasn't his problem. And she'd already caused him and his family enough grief. "Not idle threats. Stay away."

Without waiting for a response, he pivoted and returned to the bar to settle his tab. It was time to go home.

Franco and Rico were deep in discussion. Rafe was nowhere to be seen. Thank goodness. Maybe he'd taken Matt back to his place, because both brothers were gone. Marc laid a couple bills on the bar.

"Everything okay?" Luke asked as he set his long neck on the bar.

"Yeah. I'm going to head home a little early, I think." He didn't know how much Luke knew about Melissa, but Marc had no interest in filling him in.

"Is that woman going to be any trouble for you and Angel tomorrow?"

"Not if she knows what's good for her." He put his wallet away and forced a smile. "I'll see you in the morning. Thanks for being in the wedding."

"Thanks for asking. Cassie's sure excited about it."

"Is Ryder going to make it? I know crowds aren't his thing."

"He promised to try to get to the ceremony at least."

"That's above and beyond the call. Tell him we understand if he can't for any reason."

"Sure thing," Luke said, clapping him on the shoulders. "Get some sleep."

He said good night to Luke and those remaining in the bar, including Rafe, who hadn't left after all. Had Rafe seen Melissa or overheard any of their earlier conversation? Was she still skulking around? Honestly, he didn't care to check into daVinci's hiding places. Suddenly weary beyond words, he headed for the parking lot.

Marc didn't remember the drive to their recently completed log house. His mind became clouded with thoughts of what Melissa might do next. Letting himself in without turning on any of the lights, he was greeted by Lobo. The Australian shepherd mix excitedly wagged his tail, providing Marc with a bit of comfort after his run-in with his ex-fiancée. He took Lobo outside for a walk, using his phone app as a flashlight as they wandered into the woods. With each step, a sense of calm descended, and by the time he got back to the house, he was ready to feed the dog and hit the sack.

But he found a Tahoe parked in his driveway. Looked like Rafe's, although it was too dark to be certain. The tinted windows didn't allow him to see inside, but as he rounded the full-sized SUV, he could make out the shadow of a man on the porch.

"Where is she?" Rafe said without preamble.

"At your mom's with the other girls." Hadn't he paid attention at the rehearsal dinner as to what the plan was for tonight?

"Don't play stupid with me. You know who I'm talking about. I saw you two at the bar, and she left right on your tail."

"Melissa?" He hadn't seen her leave but hadn't really looked back, either.

"I don't know what her name is, but she sure as hell seemed to know you. Intimately, I would guess."

Merda. I don't need this. Not tonight.

"She's someone from my past, but it's been over between us for years, long before I met Angelina."

Rafe seemed to consider Marc's words a moment, weighing whether he'd believe them or not. Then his expression hardened. "Tony mentioned you hooking up with an old fiancée named Melissa when you and Angelina were at the resort in Aspen last year for New Year's weekend."

He wasn't about to rehash that debacle of a weekend, especially not with Angelina's overprotective big brother.

"You're barking up the wrong tree, Rafe." Remembering Lobo, he proceeded toward the door, hoping Rafe would go and leave him alone. "I need to feed the dog. I'll see you tomorrow."

"Doesn't sound like you've completely gotten her out of your life—or your blood," Rafe accused, closing in on his heels. *So much for dismissing him.* "Maybe you need to make a decision tonight which woman you want before you hurt my sister again."

Enough.

Marc spun around, close to punching his future brother-in-law in the mouth. Chest to chest, Marc clenched his fists in an attempt to keep from grabbing Rafe by the shirt and tossing him on his ass. Both men's nostrils flared as they struggled to control their anger.

But Marc had a right to be angry. Barely four hours earlier, their relatives had shared a meal in celebration of Marc and Angelina's upcoming marriage. It meant everything in the world to Angelina that her brothers accepted Marc as their families were joined. He couldn't care less whether they did or didn't like him, but seeing how far they were from trusting him to be faithful to Angelina pissed him off.

"Rafe, I don't care if you ever accept me as being good enough for Angelina. It's fine if you want to be a dick around me every time we meet, too." He narrowed his eyes and leaned closer. "But don't you *dare* doubt my love or faithfulness to Angelina ever again. There's no one else in my life, and there hasn't been since I met her."

"Prove it."

"I don't have to prove a damned thing to you, Rafe. I already proved myself to your sister. She's the one agreeing to spend the rest of her life with me and the only one who deserves it. I'll work hard to prove myself to her every single day because it's my job to make sure she never doubts or regrets her decision to marry me. But if you think she's too blind to see the *real* me or that I'm not smart enough to see what a gift she is to me, then you don't know either of us at all."

Merda! He'd spent this past year showing her brothers—Tony and Rafe, especially—that he'd changed from that lost SOB who'd made Angelina miserable over a year ago. He had his shit together ever since that interrogation scene. If he wasn't good enough for them, then fuck them all. He intended to marry their sister tomorrow afternoon. No one was getting in their way. Not Rafe. Not Melissa. *Nobody.*

"You're just going to have to trust me. Open your eyes! We love each other and want to be together for the rest of our lives. If you can't see that, then nothing I do or say is going to prove it to you," Marc finished.

"Mind if I take a look around and make sure you're alone?" Obviously, he hadn't believed a word Marc had said.

"Yeah, as a matter of fact, I *do* mind." He paused a moment before continuing. He had nothing to hide, but letting Rafe inside to search the house for Melissa wouldn't curb Rafe's distrust. "Trust starts tonight, right here and now. I'm not going to let you dog my every move for the rest of my life." If Rafe didn't get to a point where he could trust Marc, there was going to be tension between them for their entire married life. Angelina didn't need that. "Trust me, Rafe."

"Not happening."

"Then fuck off. I'm tired and going to bed." He walked past Rafe with Lobo at his side.

"Alone?"

Marc threw the first punch before he even realized he'd pivoted around. Then he followed up with another that Rafe blocked before plowing his fist into Marc's mouth.

Motherfucker, that hurt.

Marc's hand throbbed, but the two of them continued to rain blows against each other until both were out of breath and battered while Lobo barked and danced around them trying to break it up. Rafe better not leave cuts or bruises Marc would have to explain to Angelina tomorrow. She wouldn't be happy hearing he'd been fighting with her brother, although the stinging in his lower lip told him he might need to come up with a story anyway.

The crunch of tires distracted them both, and they turned to see who was coming. So much for his quiet night alone to reflect and get some damned sleep on the night before his wedding. Hunched over, with their palms resting above their knees, both men gasped to fill their lungs.

It had better not be Melissa. Otherwise, nothing Marc could say would convince Rafe they hadn't planned to meet up after their encounter at daVinci's.

Chapter Nine

B ut when Adam's SUV emerged from the woods, Marc breathed a little easier. Or tried to. How'd he gotten so out of shape? Too much time in the classroom training and not enough in the field yet, he supposed.

Adam parked near Rafe's vehicle and exited as Lobo greeted him with exuberance before chasing after something in the woods. Sauntering across the drive, his gaze went from one man to the other as he assessed the situation. "Everything okay here, Doc?"

"Yeah," Marc said, still trying to regulate his breathing. "Just burning off a little pre-wedding steam, I suppose." He'd been steamed, all right.

Adam's dubious expression told Marc he hadn't fooled the man—as if he ever could—but Marc remained quiet.

"I'd better head home," Rafe said. Was he convinced now that Melissa was nowhere to be found? Or just tired of fighting? More likely, he trusted Adam enough to believe he hadn't shown up for a threesome with Melissa.

Before Rafe could leave, Marc held out his hand, palm outward, to halt him. "This is between you and me. I don't want Angelina to hear anything about this…altercation." Marc stood straighter, already feeling the tender spot in his ribs where Rafe had landed a powerful punch. "And I don't want her to know that Melissa's in Colorado again, much less in Aspen Corners."

"Are you fucking kidding me?" Adam asked.

"No, I'm not." Marc drew a deep breath and blew it out in

disgust, wishing he could expel Melissa from his life as easily. "She's gone now. Hopefully for good this time."

"What did she want?"

"Apparently, me."

"She's not too smart, huh?" Adam chuckled. "Don't worry. I'm sure Angelina could hold her own with that one, if push came to shove."

"No doubt," Marc said. But that bitch had come between Marc and the people he loved way too many times. "I just don't want anything to mar Angelina's dream wedding. She's worked too hard to have Melissa or anyone else"—he glanced pointedly at Rafe—"raining on her big day." While it would be a momentous day for Marc, too, he was more interested in moving on to the honeymoon phase and married life.

Rafe stroked the knuckles of his right hand. "Agreed." There was also a cut on his cheek. Would they both carry bruises tomorrow? After that punch he'd landed on Marc's mouth—and his ridiculous accusations that had brought on the fight in the first place—Rafe deserved some pain and a few physical marks. "Sounds like this Melissa has tried to cause trouble before."

Marc nodded. How much of what she'd done to destroy his relationship with Gino did he want to confide to this man? Rather than hide it, he made a decision to be honest and open. With a sigh, he began. "When I was twenty-three and thinking with the wrong head, I convinced myself Melissa was the woman for me." He huffed. "*Merda*, that was some asshole thinking. I know that now but not back then. Melissa played me against my brother, costing us the final week we had together before he joined the Marines the day after 9/11 and deployed to Afghanistan. Gino was dead within six months, and I'll have to live with that for the rest of my life."

"Jesus, Marc. Sorry to hear that. I can't imagine letting a woman come between me and my brothers, but I'm a lot older than you were then."

"Ever since, Melissa's had an uncanny ability for showing up like a Biblical plague. I won't say she only turns up at the wrong time, because there's never a right time with her. Tonight, at daVinci's, I threatened her to keep her from showing up at the church or reception tomorrow, but I can't post guards at the church to keep her out."

"I know what she looks like now," Rafe said. "I'll alert my Sicilian uncles to watch for her and to neutralize any trouble she might try to cause. They'll love having a chance to throw their weight around, if need be."

"I'd appreciate that." Were Angelina's *uncles* anything like Marc's—a loose term that included older male cousins and even family friends not related by blood at all? But Italian *uncles* were known for getting shit done and for looking after their *families*. Knowing they'd be watching for trouble tomorrow would help Marc rest at ease.

However, having Rafe agree with Marc on anything was foreign territory. Still, he'd take this as a sign of cooperation with his future brother-in-law, even if the only reason he was offering was to make sure Angelina was happy. She loved her family, and Marc would be seeing a lot more of them from now on. For instance, her mama would insist he be present at more of their Sunday gatherings. He'd managed to avoid most of those dinners since their engagement, due partially to studying for his EMT certification and, more recently, working toward his paramedic one on top of his shift schedule at the Aspen Corners Fire Department. Now that he'd be married into the family, he'd probably need to make these gatherings more of a priority when he wasn't on duty. But his new brothers-in-law didn't make them all anymore, either, given their work schedules.

"So does this mean we have come to a truce?"

Marc wasn't sure until Rafe nodded. "Yeah, well, sorry I jumped to the wrong conclusions about Melissa. Since Papa died, it's been my responsibility to watch over Angelina, as well as Mama and my younger brothers. It's going to take time for me to turn those reins over to you. Love, cherish, and protect her every damned day for the rest of her life, and we'll be good."

Marc waved away his apology, knowing he'd broken that trust by hurting Angelina in the past. He accepted that he'd have to re-earn their confidence in him as her protector and intended to do just that every minute of every day. "You have my word. Let's forget tonight ever happened."

Rafe scrutinized him a moment too long then nodded. The only Giardano sibling Marc owed anything to was Angelina—and tomorrow, she'd become a D'Alessio. No way in hell would he ever let that woman down, unless it was something completely out of his control.

He couldn't wait to speak his vows loudly and proudly before her and their families and friends and to finally get on with the rest of their lives as partners for life.

* * *

"So what brings you out here tonight, Adam?" Marc asked as they watched Rafe drive away.

"Worried about you. How are you holding up?"

"Before or after getting my face punched by my soon-to-be in-law?"

Adam chuckled. "Now."

Marc whistled to Lobo before addressing his long-time friend. "Let's go inside and talk."

"Let me get my bag."

"You're spending the night?" Did he think Marc would chicken out tomorrow? As best man, did he feel it was his duty to drag him to the church?

"Yeah, well, I wasn't sure I would be until I found you and Rafe knocking the shit out of each other. You might need a wingman to get through the night since she has three other brothers who probably want to do the same."

"Nah. Rafe seems to have taken it upon himself as family patriarch to fulfill that role all by himself."

"Good. I could use a solid night's sleep."

"Babies still not good sleepers?"

"Ironically, our former Sleeping Beauty is now our non-sleeper. I hope Carl and Jenny know what they're getting into, but they insisted they wanted to take care of the triplets themselves. They're all holed up together at Gunnar's tonight. With our ladies at your mother-in-law's, I figured you could use some company."

"You know you're always welcome here. Need help with anything?"

"Nope, but we're going to do some work on that split lip and try to minimize the damage."

Marc reached up and winced when he touched it. Lobo finally came bounding out of the woods and headed straight to Marc for some loving, which he hunkered down to deliver while waiting for Adam. Carrying his seabag over one shoulder and a garment bag with his Marine dress blues for the ceremony over the other, Adam followed him into the foyer. After stowing his things in one of the guest bedrooms, Marc gave Adam a tour of the finished house. This was the first time his friend had been up here since they'd moved in.

Half an hour later, after Adam had doctored him for a change, they wound up sitting side by side on Adirondack chairs on the deck, each with a beer in hand, while looking up at the silhouette of Iron Horse Peak.

"Damn, but that's a beautiful view. And the house," Adam said, pointing his beer bottle toward the kitchen door, "turned out great."

"I wasn't sure we'd be moved in before the wedding, but we're both happy with how it turned out. Can't think of anything we'd want to fix."

"I wonder if Karla would have preferred living in the mountains over the city."

"Regardless, this house isn't for sale." They shared a laugh, but Marc wondered if Karla was unhappy with the house Marc had sold Adam. "I sure can't picture her in an isolated house in the woods like this. She's always lived in the city."

"True. Maybe we'll just rent a place like this on occasion for a getaway weekend or family vacation when the babies are older."

"You're welcome to stay here while we're on our honeymoon next week. I'm sure Karla's parents wouldn't mind watching them a few more days."

"Thanks, but I need to get back to Denver. Interviewing several potential bodyguards on Monday. A Navy SEAL and two Marines."

Adam had been working nonstop for six months on setting up his VIP security agency. Montague Security would not only bring in a new income for Adam and Karla but would also give Adam a chance to use his Marine training in a more direct way. After being active duty more than two decades, it had to be hard to shake the need to serve.

"Sounds like you're finding the vets you wanted to hire." The man was always making sure his fellow veterans were first and foremost in anything he did. "When does the agency open?"

"As soon as feasible after the Fourth of July weekend. Most of the staff is in training already, but we ought to be able to bring new team members up to speed quickly."

If anyone could pull it off in the next couple of weeks, Adam could. He'd almost single-handedly gotten the Masters at Arms Club running five years ago and had been the sole manager until the partners had turned it over to Grant's capable hands last year.

A comfortable silence ensued as each man sipped his beer. Marc used the opportunity to formulate the words he wanted to say.

"Adam, thanks for standing up with me tomorrow."

"It will be my honor."

Though not finished, Marc found himself choking up again. "Not only that, but thanks for being someone I've always been able to look up to—like a second big brother. After losing Gino, I never expected to have that kind of connection with anyone again."

Adam was quiet then cleared his throat. "Feeling's mutual. I didn't know what having a little brother was like until you joined me in starting up the club. You guys and that place saved my bacon, I'm sure. And brought Karla back to me."

"If not for the club, I'm not sure I'd have met Angelina—or if we had still shown up at daVinci's that night, whether I'd have intrigued her so much if she hadn't thought I reminded her of the phantom guy in the mask."

Adam chuckled. "I guess we both owe our happiness to that place. Damián would probably credit the club with helping him get through to Savannah after that cathartic whipping scene with Patti, too."

"Hey, I just realized something," Marc said, turning to Adam. "Today's the fifth anniversary of when we opened the doors to the Masters at Arms Club."

Adam's eyes opened wider. "I'll be damned, you're right."

"Guess we should have had a celebration or something."

The older man waved off his words. "We'll just have a double celebration in five years—the club's tenth anniversary and your fifth."

"Sounds like a plan."

They sat in silence a few minutes until Adam added, "I'm proud of the way you've unfucked your life, Doc." Marc's eyes stung at his former SNCO's praise. "That woman you're about to marry had a lot to do with turning your life around. Glad you found her. Make sure you keep her happy."

"You'd better believe I will." Marc assured him. "Every day of our lives together."

Chapter Ten

"I don't remember the back of this dress being so...revealing," Mama said.

Angelina smiled without admitting that hadn't been accidental on her part. "Marc's going to love it, isn't he?"

"Yes, I'm sure, but some things are best shared only with our husbands, not the entire congregation."

She doubted any of the countless cousins, aunts, uncles, and friends Mama and Marc's family had made sure were invited would be checking out her back anyway.

Angelina picked up the veil, knowing it would cover her back enough to distract her mother. "Help me put on your veil, Mama?" She held the cathedral-length lace and tulle creation out to her. "With all the hairspray my stylist used, you don't have to worry about messing up my hair." Marc wouldn't be happy about it, but what could she do now?

Angelina sat on the vanity bench as Megan clicked away, capturing the reflections of mother and daughter in the mirror as well as in the flesh.

The moment Mama tucked the comb of the veil onto her head, Angelina's eyes stung. When she glanced up at Mama, she saw tears in her eyes, too. Was Mama remembering her own wedding day when she'd worn this veil or thinking about Papa missing their only daughter's wedding day? *Perhaps a bit of both.*

Angelina stood and wrapped Mama in a tight embrace and whispered, "He's here with us. I can feel him."

Mama nodded, clearing her throat. "So can I."

Mama pulled away first, and Karla handed each of them a tissue before drying her own tears.

"Angie, that veil is so beautiful on you! Much prettier than the one you tried on at the salon," Karla said. Her matron of honor and the bridesmaids had dressed earlier at Mama's house, but Karla had joined her here in the tiny dressing room off the vestibule at her childhood church so that she, too, could be part of the photos taken of Angelina getting into her dress and veil.

Good thing Angelina opted for minimal makeup today—mostly some waterproof mascara and earth-tone eyeshadow—or her face would be a mess. But it felt good to let some of the tears out. This was supposed to be the happiest day of her life, and she knew Papa wouldn't want her feeling sad that he wasn't here in the flesh.

"I'll get out of your way so Megan can get more photos," Mama said. "I can't wait to see them." She cupped Angelina's cheek. "Just a few more minutes, my angel, and your groom will see you for the first time in your dress. You're the most beautiful bride in the world." Mama kissed her cheek.

"Only after you, Mama," she whispered back. Her heart squeezed tight at the thought of that moment when Marc saw her for the first time. "And have I told you yet that you look stunning in your gown?" The coral complemented the light teal color of the bridesmaids' dresses. Mama D'Alessio wore a cornflower blue formal-length dress; blue being traditional for the mother of the groom. "I noticed Paul's eyes lit up when he saw you in it."

Mama actually blushed and glanced away. She and the man she'd been seeing since the holidays seemed to be becoming serious. Watching her enjoying life again rather than sitting home grieving the loss of Papa made Angelina so happy. Her brothers, on the other hand, were a little more protective of Mama and couldn't accept her being with anyone after Papa. So far, though, Mama wasn't letting them dictate how she lived the rest of her life.

Go, Mama!

Angelina gave Mama a kiss on the cheek. "See you again in a few minutes."

After Mama left the room, no doubt to find Franco, who would escort her to her seat during the procession, Megan instructed Angelina to sit on the vanity bench again and asked Karla to remove the garter from its box. "I'm going to take some photos of you placing it on Angelina's thigh. Just follow my instructions, and we'll do it all in one take."

Angelina lifted the front of her dress's voluminous skirt into her lap. "Extend your leg toward Karla, and point your toe."

Karla hunched down and smiled as she started to slide the scrap of blue satin and white lace over Angelina's shoe and up her calf.

"That's it." *Click, click, click.* "Beautiful!"

How many photos she'd need of this, Angelina wasn't sure, but she hoped there would be twice as many taken of when Marc removed it at the reception, which would be much more exciting.

"Maybe just a little higher. Let's make Marc work for that garter."

The three of them laughed as Karla pushed the garter up to mid-thigh.

"Perfect!" Megan proclaimed. "Now, I'd better get back inside the church to prepare for the procession." She smiled at Angelina. "You're a stunning bride. More than anything else, enjoy the many precious moments throughout the day."

"I plan to! I've waited so long for this. It's almost like a dream."

"Oh, it's definitely not another wedding dream this time," Megan said as she packed up her case and left her and Karla alone. "But it will be a dream of a wedding."

"I can't believe you're getting Marc D'Alessio to the altar."

"There were some touch-and-go moments over the past two years that made me wonder if it would ever happen."

Karla laughed. "You and me both!"

"Should I send you out there in a minute to make sure Marc showed up?"

"Oh, don't think like that. Adam's primary mission is to get Marc to the church on time. Remember, no man left behind." She chuckled at her own joke. "He even spent the night with Marc since my parents were at Gunnar's with Damián and Rosa to watch over all the kids." Karla grew serious. "Honey, Marc loves you so much, and the two of you are perfect for each other. He wouldn't blow the best thing that ever happened to him unless he's a fool, which he isn't. He came too close to losing you to do anything stupid. He's got his head on straight after that horrific interrogation and has managed to sort out all the issues that have bothered him since childhood."

Well, most of them anyway. Angelina almost shuddered at the mention of that traumatic ordeal. There'd been so many times where he'd run away from her before the intervention. But she'd been the one to run after first meeting him at the club, not wanting to know who her masked wolf man was.

All that was in the past. They'd been living together for a year, and neither had found a reason or need to escape the other in that time. Nothing could derail them from taking their vows today and entering into a lifelong commitment to one another.

There was a knock at the door, and Megan popped her head in. She didn't meet Angelina's gaze but sought out Karla. "Can you call Adam and make sure everything's okay?"

No!

"They aren't here yet?" Angelina glanced at the clock on the wall, panic rising in her chest. "We're fifteen minutes away from starting."

Karla patted her hand then searched through the clutter on the vanity for her bag before pulling out her phone.

Angelina fought her old insecurities and refused to think the worst, but her first thought was that there'd been an accident or something. She watched Karla intently as she waited for Adam to accept the call, but when Karla left a voicemail message asking him to call her ASAP, Angelina's fears got the best of her.

She reached out for the phone. "Let me call Marc. I'm sure if Adam's driving he won't answer the phone."

"True!" Karla handed her the phone.

Angelina found Marc's name in Karla's favorites list and placed the call. When he answered, she let out the breath she'd been holding.

"Karla, everything's all right. We just…ran into a little speed trap on the way here."

"Marc, it's Angelina. Where are you now?"

"Don't worry, *cara*. We'll be there in five minutes tops, but we're keeping it under the speed limit the rest of the way to avoid another delay. We're both in our uniforms and ready to go."

"I was afraid there'd been an accident or something."

"I'm sorry if I worried you. I promise we'll get there safely. See you soon, *il mio amore*."

She said goodbye and ended the call then sank into the seat taking a deep breath.

"I'm giving Adam an earful for speeding," Karla said. "I wonder if they gave him a ticket. You'd think after seeing them in their uniforms and learning they were on their way to Marc's wedding, they'd thank them for their service and let them go on their way."

"You'd think." Angelina shook her head. "At worst, Adam was probably going forty in a twenty-five zone or something."

Angelina smiled at her, and Karla finally shook her head and grinned. "Whatever I decide to say to him, it won't happen until we get home from the wedding. Nothing's going to spoil your day."

Oh no! Was it bad luck for the bride to talk to her groom before the wedding, or was it only that he wasn't supposed to see her in the dress? She had considered doing the new "first look" ritual where the bride presents herself to the groom privately prior to the wedding ceremony, but Marc had insisted that the first time he saw her in her dress would be when she walked down the aisle. Angelina had to agree that sticking to tradition fit them better. Her wedding day would be very traditional in every way. While she didn't consider herself superstitious, she didn't want to tempt fate, either.

Please don't let anything go wrong today. This is going to be my dream wedding.

*   *   *

Karla had been summoned by Gina, the wedding coordinator, a moment ago, so Adam and Marc must be here.

Angelina said a little prayer for her marriage to be a long, happy union then left the room to find Rafe waiting in the vestibule dressed in his slate-gray tux. As the oldest brother, he would walk her down the aisle. He looked the most like Papa, which brought fresh tears to her eyes.

I'm sorry you missed this moment, Papa.

Rafe extended a hand to her and bent to kiss her on the cheek. *"Bellissima."*

Her heart squeezed as she imagined Papa saying the same words. She would carry him with her all day long.

"Thank you. You're quite handsome in that tux, you know." He shrugged. No doubt he wasn't comfortable in the formal attire, but he didn't complain.

"Here's your bouquet, Angie." Karla placed the holder in her hand, and she caught a whiff of the roses and orchids. "Man, are they heavy!"

Angelina smiled and nodded in agreement. She had so many favorite blossoms she didn't want to leave any out. Conversely, the girls held calla lilies wrapped in silver ribbons. Much lighter.

Karla then handed Angelina Nonna's pearl rosary—her *something old*—and she wrapped the beads around the hand holding the bouquet.

Through closed doors, Angelina heard the string trio of violin, viola, and cello playing Pachelbel's *Canon in D* as their mothers were ushered to their seats. Here at the church, they would have classical music with popular, secular songs being played by the band at the reception. All their favorite songs, music that held meaning to them both.

Gina closed the doors to the interior of the church and began lining everyone else up. After positioning Angelina midway between the church's exterior and interior doors, she guided Marisol, the flower girl, to stand in front of José, the ring bearer. They would enter just ahead of her. Karla and Carmella walked around behind Angelina and each took the hem of the dress's train to lift and fluff it out, letting it fall naturally while Megan took more photos. Next, they fluffed out her veil so that it stretched all the way to the exit doors.

When the trio began playing Vivaldi's *Spring*, the music Angelina had chosen for her bridal party's processional, she blinked away more tears.

Soon, I'll be in the arms of my one true love.

Everything was so perfect, just the way she'd imagined it would be. Maybe she was dreaming. No, she was very present in the moment and didn't intend to miss a thing.

Gina sent the bridesmaids—Carmella, Cassie, Savannah, and Pippa—down the aisle at regular intervals, followed by Karla. Marisol came next, dressed in a multitiered, white dress. So adorable, as was José in his suspenders and slate-gray dress pants with his white dress shirt. Gina handed him the sign that read "Here comes the Bride!"

Angelina smiled, knowing that Marc would read it using the other meaning of coming. She didn't want to rush the day but looked forward to their wedding night, too.

Angelina didn't catch a glimpse of Marc up front before Gina closed the doors behind José. Alone with Gina and Rafe, Angelina smiled up at him and noticed for the first time a bruise on his left cheek.

"What happened to you?" she asked, reaching up with her free hand before he grabbed her arm and stopped her from touching it.

"Ran into a door. Door won."

"Just how much drinking did you and the guys do after we left last night?"

He shrugged, making her wonder if Marc was going to be hungover when they took their vows. Surely he didn't overdo it last night, though.

Her brother took his place at her side and tucked her hand under his arm. He patted the top of her hand, surprising her with the warmth of his. She hadn't realized hers was so cold until then.

"My Tahoe's parked right out front, if you've changed your mind."

She looked up at him, incredulous he'd suggest such a thing at a time like this. Was there a twinkle in his eye, or did he mean it? A smile broke out on her face. "I love him, Rafe."

He nodded. "I can tell, baby. Just trying to lighten the mood. You seemed a little on edge a few minutes ago."

Was it that, or was he merely diverting attention from her question about his drinking binge last night? She sighed with contentment. Today was not the time to find things to worry about. "I can't believe this day has finally come."

"Won't be long now before you become Mrs. Marc D'Alessio."

Those words brought joy to her heart, and her cheeks started cramping from smiling so much. "I hope someday you'll find someone you can love the way I love Marc. Then you'll truly understand what I'm feeling."

"I have no intention of getting hitched anytime soon. I'm happy in my bachelorhood."

Was he really? She sometimes thought he was married to being a fire lieutenant in their hometown fire department. He rarely took time to date, as far as she knew. If he wasn't on duty, he was training or studying to take his vocation to the next level.

"Well, that's what they all say until the right girl comes along. I'm sure she'll have an equally overprotective father, brother, uncle, or male cousin ready to run you through a gauntlet like you did Marc. But I'll also want to make sure she's worthy of you." Tugging him down to where she could place a kiss on his cheek, she quickly wiped away the lipstick smudge. "Sorry about that."

"No need to apologize." He smiled warmly. "Ready to tie the knot?"

"More than you will ever know. Now, help me get this blusher in place, but don't forget to lift it out of the way before I join Marc. I'm going into this with my eyes open wide and want to see everything clearly."

"Yes, ma'am." He reached around her and pulled the built-in blusher over her face. She couldn't resist the air of mystery it would give her before the big reveal in front of Marc.

"How's that?" he asked.

"Perfect."

The string trio began playing Bach's "Air on the G String," and Angelina tried not to laugh at Marc's comment about the song title's double-entendre meaning when they'd first chosen it. Gina said, "And that's your cue."

"Let's go join your soon-to-be husband?" he asked.

"I've been ready to marry him for a very long time."

Gina opened the interior doors, removing the final barrier between her and Marc. When she stepped into the nave, her gaze immediately zeroed in on Marc, standing tall and handsome at the front of the church in his formal Navy uniform with a bowtie and matching trousers. While it was officially called the blue dinner jacket, it looked black to her eyes. So handsome!

The music swelled, and it was as if the world stood still, leaving only the two of them.

Mine!

With her right hand firmly tucked into the crook of his arm, Rafe started her down the aisle. She smiled continually at Marc through her blusher veil, anxious to reach his side. Marc visibly gave her the once-over—twice—his grin growing wider as well when he met her gaze again.

The spell was broken when someone's ringtone began playing "I Wish You Love," and Angelina missed a step then another. Rafe kept her upright as Dean Martin's melodic voice echoed through the church crooning a tune Papa used to sing to her at bedtime when she was young. Wishes of bluebirds in the spring and of love. She glanced up at Rafe, who seemed more annoyed at the intrusion than anything else. But in Angelina's mind, this was a sign to her that Papa was with her as she walked down the aisle. The ringtone stopped abruptly as the phone's owner silenced it, but Angelina smiled again through watery eyes.

Rafe squeezed her hand reassuringly, and she returned her gaze to Marc as she continued toward the man she'd spend the rest of her life loving. As she came closer to him, Marc beamed back at her. More tears sprang to her eyes.

At the second pew where Mama stood, they stopped. The priest recited a few words before asking who gave Angelina's hand in marriage. Rafe and Mama responded in unison, "We do."

Rafe lifted the blusher veil and laid it behind her head before placing a kiss on her cheek. Angelina walked over to kiss Mama, too.

She then faced Marc, seeing him clearly and without the tulle barrier for the first time today.

He's so beautiful. And he's all mine.

But what happened to his lower lip? It looked like it had been cut.

Marc came forward and Rafe placed her hand in Marc's, wiping all thoughts about that away—for now. When Rafe would have stepped back, Marc gave him a man hug and said in a low voice only the three of them could probably hear, "I'll always love and protect her. You can depend on that."

The two stared at each other a moment before Rafe nodded and joined Mama in the pew. They seemed to have come to some understanding. Thank God! She'd begun to lose hope for Rafe ever accepting her intended.

Marc walked her the rest of the way to where the priest awaited them in front of the altar.

At last. There'd been days when she never thought they'd make it this far, but here they were.

Chapter Eleven

A lump formed in Marc's throat the moment his gorgeous bride appeared in the doorway at the back of the church. Her beautiful dress, veil, and flowers added to the picture burned into his mind forever, but when the veil had been lifted, he couldn't take his eyes off her face. Swallowing hard against the lump in his throat, he hoped he'd be able to speak when the time came to say those long-overdue, all-important words that would bind him to Angelina's side for the rest of their lives.

He accepted her hand from Rafe, whom Marc bro-hugged before leading her to stand beside him in front of the priest. Angelina handed her bouquet and rosary to Karla.

Cara, I won't let you down, he vowed silently.

When she trembled, he placed his hand over hers to warm it. After making the sign of the cross, the priest offered up a prayer and the *Gloria* before he indicated that Marc and Angelina should take their seats.

As quietly and unobtrusively as possible, he whispered, "You look stunning today, *il mio amore*." When she'd walked into the church, she'd worn the biggest smile he'd ever seen on her face. Even the unexpected Dean Martin ringtone hadn't dampened her spirits. If anything, her smile became radiant at that point, no doubt thinking about her father making his presence known.

"I love you, Marc," she whispered between the readings.

His chest swelled with pride hearing her words. That this gorgeous woman had consented to become his wife still floored him when he allowed the thought to sink in. Nothing and no one would ever come between them. Today was the beginning of a new phase in their relationship, one that would continue beyond this lifetime for all eternity.

After the priest gave the homily, he invited everyone to stand and for the bride, groom, and wedding party to come before him again. Marc helped Angelina to her feet, and Karla and Carmela arranged her train before taking their places beside her.

Angelina beamed a radiant smile up at him, even bigger than the one she'd given him when she entered the church. Both of them were going into this marriage wholeheartedly without any reservations.

"Marco, I love you! Don't make this terrible mistake!"

Merda. What the fuck was that bitch doing here?

Angelina gasped, and he squeezed her hand reassuringly. He glanced over her shoulder to where Rafe sat. Rafe gave a nod toward someone in the back of the church.

"Take your hands off me. Who do you think you are?" Rafe gave Marc a sign that all would be okay. "Mar—" Melissa's voice became muffled, and then he heard the sound of the doors at the back being shut.

Well done, Rafe.

"How *dare* she?" Angelina whispered.

"Forget about her. She's gone." It had better be for good this time. That bitch had been warned not to come anywhere near Angelina today. If Rafe's uncles didn't take care of her, Marc would, but he'd rather not upset Angelina by causing a scene. Melissa had some nerve to think she'd be welcomed here—or delusional if she thought he'd choose her over his treasure, Angelina. More likely, she simply wanted to stir up trouble—yet again. But he wouldn't allow anything to mar this beautiful day. Melissa's days of disrupting their lives were over. She'd caused enough harm to his family already. He reined in his own thoughts and brought himself back to this moment, banishing Melissa to a bottomless pit far away from either of them.

Marc gave the stunned priest a nod after the murmurings in the church died down. "Father, we're ready to continue if you are."

The priest cleared his throat. "Dearly beloved, you have come together before God and these witnesses so that…" Marc forced himself to focus on the ceremony, forgetting about the momentary distraction. "I ask you both to state your intentions," Father Bancroft said.

The priest questioned them again about their freedom of choice, fidelity to one another, and the acceptance and upbringing of children. He then asked, "Angelina and Marco, have you come here to enter into marriage without coercion, freely and wholeheart-edly?"

Simultaneously, they answered, "I have."

When it came time for them to say their vows, Father said, "Please join your right hands and repeat after me."

The lump in his throat trapped his words, and he had to start again. "I, Marco Zirilli D'Alessio, take you, Angelina Cristina Giardano, to be my wife. I promise to be faithful to you, in good times and in bad, in sickness and in health, to love you and to honor you all the days of my life."

Dio, let that be an incredibly long time because I have a lot of mistakes to make up for.

While he'd heard those words spoken before by others at numerous weddings, they took on an importance he'd never forget or take for granted. Hearing Angelina speak her vows after him in a quavering voice made him see all the more than he was the absolute luckiest man in the world.

"What God joins together, no one may put asunder."

Adam and Karla were asked to present the rings to the priest. He prayed over and blessed them with holy water then gave Marc and Angelina each other's ring. Marc placed Angelina's on her finger first. Seeing the band of platinum on her slim finger gave him pause. This would be a daily reminder of his commitment to her and to their marriage. He would proudly wear the ring she was about to place on his finger that announced to the world that he was Angelina's husband.

"Marc, receive this ring as a sign of my love and fidelity. In the name of the Father, the Son, and the Holy Spirit." She slipped the matching ring onto his finger and smiled up at him.

As the Mass continued, they knelt before the altar, exchanging glances and furtive smiles throughout. After Communion and the conclusion of the Mass, they were asked to stand once more, and Father Bancroft prayed a blessing over them, their marriage, and all those present.

"I now pronounce you husband and wife. Marco, you may kiss your bride."

About damned time.

He faced his lovely bride and lowered his mouth to hers, claiming her lips in their first searing kiss as a married couple. Someone on the bride's side—Rafe no doubt—cleared his throat, indicating he should cut the kiss shorter than Marc wanted to. Marc ignored him.

Finally, when he was ready, Marc pulled away, but quickly captured her lips in another kiss to the laughter of many in the church.

"If you're finished, Marco," Father Bancroft said with a smile, "please turn and face the congregation." They did, holding hands, and the priest went on to say, "Let me be the first to introduce Marco and Angelina D'Alessio."

A round of applause greeted them before they were instructed to begin the wedding party's recessional as the celebratory strains of Jeremiah Clarke's *Trumpet Voluntary* played.

Tugging her into a corner of the vestibule, he wasted no time pulling her into his arms for another kiss. *Dio*, he'd never get enough of this woman.

When others intruded to offer congratulations, they were separated as Angelina's friends and family hugged her and asked to see her ring. Catching Rafe out of earshot of Angelina, he said in a low voice, "Melissa's taken care of, I presume."

"Absolutely." Rafe grinned. "My Sicilian uncles would have felt useless if she hadn't shown up to give them a situation to handle."

"I hope you're right. I'm always so sure she's gone forever… Then she turns up again."

"She won't be back. Trust me. She's gone for good."

A sudden thought hit him about whether Angelina's family included members of the infamous *Cosa Nostra,* but he discarded them. She'd have told him if she had mob connections. Wouldn't she? More likely, they were typical overprotective Italian "uncles." But if Melissa put *Sicilian* and *family* together and came up with the Mafia, that might be what it took to put the fear of God in her. Maybe they had heard the last from her once and for all time.

As Rafe went to check on his mother, Marc gave him a silent salute for handling the situation with efficiency and very little drama. Both Marc and Rafe loved Angelina and wanted only what was best for her. Perhaps this truce with Rafe would develop into a strong familial bond. Being on the same side of an issue seemed to make all the difference.

"Marco," Father Bancroft interrupted his thoughts, "If you'll gather your witnesses, it's time for them to sign the license before we finish up photos and you hurry off to your reception. Then we'll all sign a commemorative certificate of marriage that you can take home with you." They'd already made plans to have it professionally framed to hang in a prominent place in their new home.

"Yes, Father. Excuse me a moment." He returned to Angelina, who was surrounded by some of her family and her bridesmaids. "Pardon me while I steal this woman," he said to everyone. "Karla, if you and Adam will join us to sign some papers," he said, pointing out where Father Bancroft had gone. Marc gently took Angelina's arm and led to where the priest awaited them.

After signing the various documents, Adam and Karla went out to round up the wedding party and key family members for the post-ceremony posed photos. The priest picked up the official license to record it with the county clerk's office. "Congratulations, and long life to you both."

"Are you sure you don't want to board the bus for the reception, Father?" Angelina asked.

The priest chuckled but shook his head. "Italian wedding receptions are a younger man's game." After saying goodbye and receiving their thanks once more, the priest left them alone. Pulling Angelina into his arms, Marc couldn't resist another kiss. Would he ever have his fill of her?

Not for a thousand years, give or take a few.

After the bare minimum of posed post-ceremony photos, they were ready to head to Aspen for the reception. Stepping outside the church, a quick scan of the area didn't show any sign of Melissa. Thank God.

They soon were enveloped in a sea of bubbles being blown by their guests, and all thoughts of that woman were banished from his mind. "*Bacio! Bacio!*" a few of the Sicilian men shouted.

As if he needed to be prompted, sore lip or not. "If you insist," Marc said, pulling Angelina into his arms for the kiss their guests demanded. Framing her face, he looked into her eyes and saw nothing but love, which was all he'd ever need to see.

"I love you, Mrs. D'Alessio."

"I love you back, Mr. D'Alessio."

And he kissed her. Then again, for good measure.

When he pulled away, she slowly licked her bottom lip, not breaking eye contact with him, as if no one else existed and she couldn't get enough of the taste of him.

Merda! If only they could skip over the reception and head straight to the honeymoon suite for the night. During the hour-long limo ride to the resort—alone because members of the wedding party were driving themselves and their families—he intended to kiss her one or two hundred more times.

The salute of bubbles continued all the way down the church steps and into the waiting limo. Inside, the magnum of champagne he'd ordered was chilling in an ice bucket. He popped the cork and poured each of them a flute before the driver pulled away from the curb.

"May our perfect wedding day lead to an even more perfect marriage," he toasted. They clinked glasses and each took a sip.

"That's it for me. I don't have anything in my stomach."

"You didn't eat breakfast?"

"Couldn't. Too nervous."

Marc couldn't contain the growl that emitted from his throat but had expected as much. He leaned over and opened the mini-fridge, pulling out a tray of cheese and another of strawberries. He pulled off the stem of one of the berries and plopped it into her glass then did the same with his. Then he held the stem of another and brought it to her lips. "Eat."

"Wait." She removed her veil, setting it on the opposite bench seat, and grabbed a cloth napkin to cover the bodice of her dress before resuming the position and accepting his offering into her mouth. He watched her chew slowly, sensuously, again keeping her gaze on his. His cock twitched in anticipation of what was to come. While they had the privacy in here to make love the entire trip to Aspen, he didn't think he'd be able to keep her dress pristine for the reception and didn't want to spoil it for her.

They had a little more than a week to themselves—no jobs, no responsibilities—just them.

After she'd eaten a few more berries and some cubes of cheese, she leaned back against the seat, closing her eyes. "That was so good. Thank you. And what a perfect day it's been so far." Suddenly, her eyes shot open, and she speared him. "Except for one thing. What the hell was Melissa the Bitch thinking crashing our wedding like that?"

He shrugged. "I can't attest to her motives, but your Sicilian uncles took care of her."

"How'd they know to step in so quickly? She hardly got started before they were hauling her out."

Marc shrugged. If he mentioned Rafe's involvement in tipping them off, he'd have to explain how Rafe knew to expect Melissa, but he didn't intend to bring up what happened last night for a long while. "Don't all Italian uncles step in and handle messy issues for their loved ones?"

She blinked a few times, as if considering his words. "I suppose so." Then more resolutely, "Yeah, come to think of it, they always did things like that for Nonna, too."

"Don't give that bitch another thought, *amore*. She'll never bother either of us again. Your uncles were quite persuasive, from what I hear, that it would be detrimental to her well-being to ever bother us again. I don't know or care where she'll end up, but she's out of our lives forever this time. I'm confident."

She smiled as she lifted her glass again and held it in the air for a toast.

"To overprotective uncles and family bonds!"

After both took another sip, he decided to divert her from further thoughts about Melissa and get an answer to a question he was curious about. "Tell me, though, so I don't say the wrong thing around them. Does *family* have a more sinister meaning for your Sicilian uncles?"

She swatted his arm. "Don't tease about something like that. Of course they aren't *Cosa Nostra*. You've watched too many movies about Sicilians. Nonna had an aversion to the mob and would haunt anyone in the family who became associated with them."

Silly as it might seem, he breathed a sigh of relief. He'd love her family, no matter what they did, but they'd be a little easier to love without the criminal activity.

"While we're asking questions, is it a coincidence that you and Rafe are both sporting facial injuries this morning?"

He shrugged. "I didn't notice anything. What did he say about it?"

"That he ran into a door."

Marc grinned, pleased that Rafe hadn't spilled the beans, either. "Completely plausible. We all had a little too much to drink after you left last night." Marc had no intention of bringing Angelina into the middle of it. They'd handled things in their own way.

She studied the cut on his lip a moment longer before curling up against him and splaying her hand on his dress coat, fiddling with the buttons. Did she buy their explanations? He hoped so. Seemed like he'd started to win over his new brother-in-law, too, which made him happy.

He'd know for sure after interactions with Rafe at the reception.

Wrapping her in his embrace, he placed his hand on her lower back and connected with skin. Stroking upward, there was even more skin, reminding him of the first night they'd danced.

He set her away from him. "Turn around."

With a sly grin, she did so, and he took in the expanse of flesh visible in her backless gown. "*Merda*, you've been holding out on me. That's the hottest wedding dress I've ever seen."

Glancing over her shoulder, she grinned. "I knew you'd love it."

"Seeing your sexy back like that is going to make the next few hours interminable. Are you sure we can't ditch the reception and head straight to the honeymoon suite?"

She swatted his shoulder as she turned back around. "If you think my uncles are proficient at taking care of problems, just wait until my mama bangs on our door and demands that we get ourselves down to the ballroom immediately."

He could almost picture the little spitfire that was her mother doing just that.

"I guess both our families put a lot into planning this event."

She nodded. "We can't let them down."

Pulling her into his embrace again, he rested his chin on the top of her hair, as if she could mess it up with all the hairspray, but he needed to have her close. "I'll find the self-discipline to make it through until we've done our duty."

"Oh, Marc. You make it sound like it's going to be torture. This is our party, and I, for one, intend to have a lot of fun with it!"

Chapter Twelve

A t the head table, his gorgeous bride placed a hand on his knee and short-circuited his brain. Angelina leaned over and asked, "Who *are* all these people? There are so many more than we had RSVPs for."

Marc tore his gaze away from her long enough to survey the largest ballroom at his parents' resort. It was filled to capacity already, but staff were setting up two more rounds of ten at the back of the room to accommodate some guests still standing near the entrance. "I thought you knew them."

"I'll have to assume they just didn't send back their RSVP, because I didn't know most of the people on the list in the first place." Angelina's stomach churned. "But we didn't order enough food for so many unexpected guests."

"Don't worry. This is an Italian-run resort. Carmella knows how Italian families are at weddings. We won't run out of food or space to accommodate any crashers."

"Are you sure?"

"Absolutely positive."

"Regardless, I won't be able to eat a bite," Angelina said.

Marc cupped her chin and forced her to meet his Dom stare. "This is our wedding day. Everything is perfect. This is also our first meal together as husband and wife, and we *both* are going to participate fully in this feast. This resort has never run out of food for any event I'm aware of, but you can be certain that Mama and Carmella aren't going to let anyone leave hungry." He hated seeing the worry lines still wrinkling her forehead.

"Look, if it would help you enjoy yourself more, I can speak with Chef Renaldo."

"Please apologize to him for me."

He tapped her on the nose when what he'd like to do is give her a good anxiety-reducing spanking. "You did nothing wrong. The only ones who should apologize are the crashers."

"At this point, I don't even know who RSVP'd and who didn't."

"Likewise."

When Marc returned to the head table, the staff began serving Angelina and the wedding party their *aperitivo* before moving on to the guests at the tables surrounding the dance floor. He passed along to Angelina Chef Renaldo's assurances that a couple dozen more people would be no problem. He had anticipated such, just as Marc had tried to assure his bride who had a need to serve and take care of everyone. But that was one of the traits he loved most about her.

She beamed up at him. "Thank you for checking on things, sweetheart. Now, let's enjoy this amazing meal."

When that course was being cleared, Adam tapped his knife against his glass of prosecco and stood.

"I want to thank everyone who came from far and near to celebrate and bring added joy to Marc and Angelina's day. As you can see, they've been floating on a cloud all day." He cleared his throat before continuing. "I've watched the attraction between them grow from the day they met."

Marc hoped that those who thought they'd first met at daVinci's didn't question how Adam had been present there, not knowing Adam referred to the night Marc rescued Angelina from the abusive fake Dom. But Adam really had been there from the beginning, even though he'd refused to divulge Angelina's address to him when Marc had wanted to get in touch with her again. If not for that chance meeting in daVinci's a month later...

"Like all couples, they've had their ups and downs—although maybe a little more lively given their Italian heritage." Good-natured laughter filled the room. "But you can't deny true love when it hits you in the gut, and these two have the real deal. They've both fought like hell to get where they are today, and now they have the best days of their lives ahead of them."

Adam raised his glass, and everyone in the room did the same. *"Cent'anni! Salute! Evviva gli sposi!"*

Wow! Adam must have been practicing the traditional Italian toast delivered by the best man, because he'd nailed it, albeit with an upper Midwest American accent. As a courtesy to his fellow non-Italians in the room, though, he immediately followed with, *"A hundred years! Good health! Long live the bride and groom!"*

The room erupted into a chorus of cheers as they drank to Adam's toast of well-wishes. Then the guests began clinking their glasses in unison, prompting Marc to help his bride to her feet. Curling his fingers around the nape of her neck, he pulled her toward him. Her lips tasted of wine and Angelina's essence. As he deepened the kiss with his tongue, laughter erupted in the room. Angelina pulled away, blushing, but the sparkle in her eyes warmed him to his soul.

"I'll never let you down, *mio angelo.*"

"Nor I, you."

The *primo* was served, including the pasta Angelina and her staff had made a few days ago. Marc glanced toward his mother who beamed as she spoke animatedly with those at her table, gesturing to her plate of pasta. Mama wasn't generous with her praise but clearly was impressed with Angelina's culinary skills once again.

"I've never seen my mama so radiant," Angelina said. Moving the reception to the resort had been the right decision, even if it bucked tradition. Mama G and her four sons had all pitched in to make sure the costs were covered by the Giardano family. Carmella and Sandro had quietly insisted on giving them the family discount, but Angelina and Marc kept that to themselves. No one had lost face. Seeing both their mamas beaming and enjoying themselves made Marc happy, too.

The meal progressed to the *dolce* being served while Tony gave a playful toast. Baby brother held no intimidation over Marc, although any of her brothers would have his ass in a sling at the slightest inkling that Angelina was unhappy.

With the meal complete, the musicians indicated it was time for him to take his bride to the dance floor. He'd chosen to surprise her on their first dance with a song he first heard by Swiss singer Caroline Chevin in a cover for Donny Hathaway's "A Song for You." He might not be able to sing it to her without hurting her eardrums, but as the music and lyrics moved into the second stanza and wrapped around them, she glanced up at him in tears.

"Oh, Marc, I'll always see the best part of you—the man I know you to be."

He pulled her closer, resting his head on the top of hers as he hoped he had a long life to show her how much he loved her. The song held meaning for him about what he'd put her through but that he vowed to worship and adore her the rest of their lives. She'd pulled him out of hiding at last, and he had no intention of ever going back to that dark place.

*   *   *

Angelina was moved to tears by the song Marc had chosen for their first dance as husband and wife. Over time, she hoped he'd learn that she'd forgiven him long ago. And that it didn't matter what anyone else thought. They knew what they had was right for them.

"No more hiding for you," she said to him after the song ended.

"No more hiding."

Before the music faded on their first dance, Marc stopped moving preparing to step back.

"We're not finished yet. I chose a song for you, too."

Immediately, the band went into *Questo Amore*, by the Italian operatic pop trio Il Volo. While Marc preferred classical opera, this song spoke to her, and she hoped Marc would take the lyrics to heart. She hadn't any remaining doubts or questions and hadn't in a long time.

As the music ended, she looked up at Marc whose eyes shimmered with unshed tears. She reached up to brush his cheek. "I want you the way you are, Marc. And without a doubt, we will share infinite happiness."

"Bacio!" one of her Sicilian relatives shouted.

Marc leaned down to capture her lips in a kiss that made her toes curl, but it was broken off too soon. Angelina looked up to see Rafe standing behind him, cutting in. Tears sprang to her eyes when the opening strains of "I Wish You Love," one of Papa's favorite Dean Martin tunes, began to play. She hadn't selected it, fearful it might leave her a blubbering mess, just as it almost had when someone's ringtone played it during her processional. Had Rafe chosen it ahead of time or only after seeing how much it meant to her earlier today?

Rafe was sweet for wanting to do the father-daughter dance with her, but she'd intended to skip that part of the rituals tonight. Her heart hurt too much, and there could be no substitute for Papa.

But before she could decline his invitation to dance, Marc kissed her cheek and stepped back, extending her hand to her oldest brother. While she wouldn't be dancing with Papa tonight, she decided to pretend and let his memory surround her heart with warmth.

Angelina's cheeks were wet by the time she laid her head against Rafe's shoulder. "Papa's here," he whispered. "Can you feel him?"

She nodded, unable to speak at first, but she cleared her throat after a moment and gained her composure. "I've felt him all day."

"Remember, I'm just a stand-in tonight. Let the music and words move through you while thinking about Papa."

They glided around the dance floor, and she pretended she was dancing with Papa again. Suddenly, her father's voice came through the speakers. "Here's my beautiful angel." Her mind flashed back to a Christmas school pageant in which she'd been dressed as one of the angels. Papa had been recording the event on his enormous VHS video recorder. She pulled away to meet Rafe's gaze with both wonder and confusion. Clearly, he'd planned this well in advance.

"Just listen, baby." He resumed the dance steps, pulling her against him once more so that she couldn't see his face and could better imagine Papa. Overcome with emotion, she squeezed him to her and listened as Papa's voice mingled with the song's lyrics. "Look at how beautiful my little angel dances." Mama had videotaped Papa's dance lessons as he prepared her for her first school dance. She'd been a clumsy mess, but Papa never saw mistakes in anything Angelina had ever done.

Rafe stopped. Her eyes brimmed with tears. She hated for this moment to come to an end, but then she saw her second-oldest brother waiting to cut in and continue the dance.

"Allow me," Franco said. Without a word, she moved into his arms.

Papa's voice kept coming through the speakers. "I might not always be with you, *Angelina mia*, but I'll be forever in your heart." She didn't recall a memory to match up to those words. It was almost as if he'd truly broken through the veil and joined them here tonight.

Matteo cut in next, and the song changed to "Return to Me." If only Papa could. It had been nine years last month since he'd been taken away from them. "You'll always be Papa's little girl," Matteo said.

She nodded. "I miss him so much."

"I know, sweetie. We all do."

He held her closer as they floated around the dance floor. Papa said, "You're so beautiful, Angelina." He told her that almost every day. "I love you, sweetheart."

Just when she thought she'd become a blubbering mess as her grief and longing hit full force, the tempo of the music changed to the rapid beat of "Sway" *as* Tony cut in.

"Let's show 'em some more of the moves Papa taught you," he whispered. Leave it to Tony to lift her spirits. He always did.

While she'd struggled with the rumba all those years ago, when she closed her eyes and pictured Papa spinning her around the dance floor, her feet miraculously did what they were supposed to do. As if possessed, in her mind's eye at least, she nailed it. The beat pounded through her, and she laughed with exuberance as they executed the rapid footwork before he lowered her in a graceful dip at the finale.

She opened her eyes to find Tony grinning down at her. He set her back on her feet just as Marc came to reclaim her.

"You're amazing to watch, *cara*. I had no idea you could dance like that."

She laughed, a sparkle in her eyes. "Neither did I! I was inspired by Papa." Her melancholy mood from the beginning of the dance had been replaced by one of so much joy.

He framed her upturned face and lowered his mouth to hers for a tender kiss. "Your brothers are amazing to do that for you."

"Yes, they are!"

Angelina broke away and hugged each brother in turn, thanking them for such a heartwarming gift.

Chapter Thirteen

Somewhat thrown off the game plan, Angelina turned to Mama to see what was supposed to happen next. Mama motioned for Angelina to escort Marc to his mama.

At her husband's side, before Angelina could tell him where he needed to be, he asked, "How much longer do we have to stay here?" he whispered, nibbling her earlobe. "I want you in my bed as soon as possible."

She shook her head. "Hang on a little while longer, lover boy. We'll be here until the bitter end. Now, you need to dance with Mama D."

"I'd rather dance with you," he said only loud enough for her to hear as he placed a string of kisses down the column of her neck, but she cut him short by pulling away and facing him. "Go! She's waiting." She pushed him in her direction.

"Yes, *cara*."

She went over to the band and told them it was time to play the song he'd chosen for his dance with his mama.

They'd listened to dozens of songs in the past few months, searching for the one to best express what Marc had to convey to Mama D'Alessio. He'd had tears in his eyes the moment this one played on YouTube, signaling they'd found the perfect song. Angelina got goosebumps as the violins began to play the haunting melody to "You Raise Me Up."

Watching him dance with Mama D'Alessio filled Angelina with emotion. This woman had indeed raised him up to stand on mountains and walk on stormy seas, even though in his early years she'd had to give him to another to raise. It warmed Angelina's heart knowing he'd finally come to accept the circumstances of his birth and the woman who had sacrificed so much of herself to give him a good life. Uncovering the truth had nearly cost Marc his sanity, but in the end, the tumultuous journey had brought him closer than ever to his parents.

As the music ended, Marc placed a kiss on both of Mama's tearstained cheeks before Papa tapped him on the shoulder to cut in. Marc gave the man who'd raised him a hug before extending Mama's hand to him as other couples converged on the dance floor.

Thankfully, the emotionally charged traditional wedding dances were behind them, and they could move into more playful dancing. Over the next half hour, she danced with Papa D'Alessio, Sandro, and even did some boot-scooting boogieing with Luke. Marc was kept busy as well dancing with her mama, Carmella, and Cassie.

While taking a break to grab a glass of water, Angelina thought about what was still to come tonight when those willing and able would dance the tarantella. While Marc's family was northern Italian, Angelina had been taught the conga-line-like dance by Nonna. Her grandmother and her Sicilian-born siblings and cousins had grown up with the traditional dance. When the time came, Angelina would picture Nonna among the guests as they executed the joyful steps at her wedding reception.

"May I have this dance?"

Angelina turned to find Adam standing there, as dashing as ever in his dress blues, but still oh so intimidating. This man was such an important part of Marc's life, but Angelina never thought she measured up in his eyes.

Don't let him think you're afraid of him.

Accepting his hand, she said with false bravado, "Of course!"

The band's female vocalist came up to the mic and began singing "I'll Be There." Her delivery rivaled Mariah Carey's rendition that Angelina adored.

"I've never seen Marc as happy as he's been since you guys got back from Italy last year."

They'd gotten engaged on the flight home. So much of her world had been altered by that moment. "He's brought me a lot of joy, too."

"Not that he didn't put you through a lot of shit to get there."

She laughed aloud, surprised at this turn of events. "I won't disagree with you there." She sobered. "But Marc's a good man, despite his flaws." *And insecurities.* "And he's the only man I can see myself spending the rest of my life with."

Adam nodded. "None of us have given our girls an easy time of it." He glanced to her left to where she saw Marc and Karla dancing before returning his focus on Angelina. "But I knew you were the one for him long before he got his head out…opened his eyes."

"Really? When was that?"

"The night you came barging into the dungeon demanding to see him during that interrogation scene from hell."

She couldn't prevent the shudder from going through her body at the memory of that horrific day. He'd looked so broken, body and soul.

Returning to the conversation, she said, "I got the distinct impression you were more than a little pissed at me for showing up uninvited."

He laughed. "Damn right, I was." His smile faded. "But if you hadn't been able to understand his childish Italian gibberish, I'm not sure we'd have known what was going on with him. And Lord knows my skills at aftercare would have been sorry in comparison to yours. You two are just made for each other, even if it did take him a while to figure it out."

Having Adam's approval and vote of confidence made her eyes sting. "Thank you."

"I also wanted to commend you for supporting him in his decision to become an EMT. He was a damn good corpsman, and I know he's going to make a difference serving his community this way."

"He already has. Did he tell you he started training to become a paramedic?" Adam nodded. "He has about two more semesters of classes to go, but I'm thrilled that he's found his calling."

"Now's the time to do it, before any little D'Alessios show up. Believe me, they will tie you both down more than you can imagine."

She knew Adam wouldn't change a thing about his triplets.

"I'm sure. And coming from a firefighting family, I know what the job entails for family members. Just like military spouses having to watch loved ones go into dangerous situations, I'm not going to say it's been easy. But I know he and my brothers train hard and take every precaution to give them the best chance to return home after each shift."

Not that they could control every situation. Papa had trained hard, too, and served for many years. There were no guarantees in life. But she didn't want to dwell on anything negative tonight.

When the music came to an end, Adam seemed reluctant to part just yet. She waited for him to say what else was on his mind. After a few moments, he did.

"Angelina, you've earned your spot in my extended family. Hell, I'd have welcomed you with or without being Marc's woman—just for teaching Karla how to cook." She giggled, appreciating that he'd broken the tension. "If you ever need anything—and I do mean *anything*—you can come to me."

"Thanks so much, Adam."

"But I'm glad I have you on duty to watch over that moody Italian of yours. Just keep loving him the way you have so far. You're going to make a huge impact on his life for decades to come."

"And he on mine."

Adam bent to kiss her on the cheek, and this time the tears didn't stay contained. To be welcomed into Adam's Masters at Arms Club family, not to mention his military one, meant the world to her.

"Thank you, Adam, for bringing him back from Iraq and giving him a new purpose in life. Knowing you'll have both our backs is so reassuring."

The future looked bright for her and Marc. They'd each found their professional calling, and despite busy days apart, they always fell into each other's arms at the doorway each night. In a few years, they would welcome a passel of children into their happy union. *God willing.* Angelina sometimes wondered how she hadn't gotten pregnant already, given how many times they'd been careless about protection, but she probably had an angel on her shoulder making sure the timing would be right—once they were more established in their new careers.

"What are you grinning about?" Marc asked her as she watched Adam return to Karla's side and escort her back to their table.

"Just thinking about something Adam said to me."

He narrowed his gaze. "Are you two plotting against me?"

She giggled. "No! Of course not."

Marc leaned closer and whispered, "The only thing I want you plotting is our escape from this reception so we can start the honeymoon phase."

"It won't be much longer, sweetheart." She scanned the room trying to think what came next then turned back to him. "You still haven't told me where we're going."

"A man has to keep his wife guessing to keep the spark alive."

"Oh, I have no doubt in my mind that we are going to have plenty of spark for the next seventy years, give or take a decade or two."

"Don't keep me guessing. What's next on the agenda?"

"Greeting our guests at each table and sharing the trays of

cookies Mama and I baked."

"Let's do it."

Drawing Marc to the cookie-covered table in the corner, Angelina noted where the small drawstring bags had been placed for guests to take a few extra cookies home. A white Victorian birdcage in the corner had been stuffed with cards, Angelina's answer to Mama's wanting them to go around at the reception carrying a satin purse to collect cash gifts or, worse yet, do the embarrassing money dance.

However, Angelina had poured her heart and soul into cookie baking, because she didn't want to leave out any of their families' food-oriented traditions. She and Mama had spent days in Mama's kitchen making hundreds of Florentine lace, *pignoli*, and iced anise-flavored cookies.

Marc picked up one tray of the assorted family favorites and she another before making their way to their guests. They stopped first at the table where the Orlandos, Dentons, Pippa, Dr. Mac, Rosa, and her children were seated. Marisol and José had been allowed to stay up late to enjoy the party. Marisol looked so grown up. Glittery sparkles had been scattered in her upswept hair giving her a fairylike appearance.

"You're the prettiest bride since Maman," Marisol told her.

Angelina smiled. "That's a very high compliment. Thank you. And you look like a fairy princess." Marisol beamed as her daddy patted her shoulder, smiling down at his daughter with so much pride and joy. Angelina could imagine Damián and Savannah picturing her *quinceañera*. Even though her fifteenth birthday was six years off, she was growing up so fast.

"Would you like some cookies?" she asked Marisol, remembering the other reason why she was making the rounds. "My mama and I baked them just for our guests." After explaining what was in each of them, more or less, Marisol filled her plate with one of each and the adults followed suit.

Angelina noticed Savannah looked more at peace now that the trial was behind her. She patted the back of her healthy baby boy, J.D., after having fed him recently. After all the woman had been through in her life, she'd earned a long patch of smooth sailing for a change.

"Everything has been so beautiful," Savannah said. "My wish for you both is that today is the beginning of a life filled with happiness, love, and adventure."

"Thank you, *cara*," Marc said, smiling down at Angelina. "With this woman by my side, we're in for quite an adventure."

Angelina laughed. "But one we both welcome."

"Agreed," he said.

At the next table were the Montagues, Grant, Gunnar, and Sergeant Miller's widow, three children, and her new husband. This was the first time Angelina had a chance to chat with Claire or to meet her kids.

"Congratulations, Marc and Angelina. What a beautiful wedding," she said, smiling at them.

"I hear congratulations also are in order for you and Tyler as well," Angelina said.

The love shining from Claire's face as she smiled at her husband of just a few months must give Adam and the others who served with the sergeant great joy and a sense of well-being, knowing she'd found love again after losing her husband in Iraq.

"They'll be staying with us for the coming week," Adam said, "while Tracy gets a sneak peek at the University of Denver before classes start in August." She'd seen Tracy was hanging out with Teresa Espinosa, Damián's niece. The two were about the same age and might even become friends while living in Denver.

"Just knowing there will be members of our Marine family close by when my baby is so far from home puts my heart at ease."

"Don't you worry, Claire," Adam said. "Damián and I are usually here in town. If not, one of the agents in my security firm will be available. We'll keep an eye on her and make sure she knows all our phone numbers."

After doing her spiel about the cookies and making sure everyone had taken plenty of samples, she added, "Be sure to go to the cookie table before you leave and fill up bags of your favorites to take home."

Marc and Angelina thanked Adam and Karla again for being such an important part of their wedding day before moving on. It took them nearly an hour to go to every table, after returning to the cookie table to restock numerous times, but at last, they'd thanked everyone. Marc placed a kiss at the place where her neck and shoulder met.

Her breath caught in her chest. "Why don't we move on to cutting the cake and up our departure time a little?"

"I thought you'd never ask."

*   *   *

While Marc showed restraint when it came to feeding Angelina the cake, she was not so inclined and smashed the amaretto-flavored piece against his lips and chin. For that, she would pay—but not until they were in their honeymoon suite tonight. He'd have her covered in cake by midnight—and would lick each and every bite off of her.

Turning to the baker who was serving the cake, Marc said, "Nicolo, please see that the rest of this top layer of cake is delivered to our suite tonight."

"Yes, sir."

"Thank you." Marc accepted a cloth napkin from the baker's assistant and wiped his face.

"What on earth are we going to do with that much cake, husband?"

His smoldering gaze must have conveyed to her his carnal thoughts, because her eyes opened wider. "You wouldn't."

"Is that a challenge?"

"No. But will you at least let me get out of my dress first?"

"Depends."

"On what?"

"On how long you make me stay at this reception."

"Stop complaining and remove my garter then."

"Love to, but aren't you supposed to toss the bouquet first?"

"Oh, yeah. You have me a little flustered, that's all."

As if on cue, the master of ceremonies called the single women and young girls to the dance floor. Marc recognized Sergeant Miller's daughter, Tracy. She was joined by Teresa, several Giardano and D'Alessio cousins, Carmella, one of the hostesses at Angelina's restaurant, and a dozen or so other girls. Grant was making a hasty retreat into the crowd and away from the dance floor, apparently not interested in participating in the silly tradition. He couldn't blame her.

Franco urged Mama Giardano to join them. Angelina had told him she'd been dating the man for six months now. Judging by the way Marc had seen them dancing earlier, she seemed serious about him. He wondered if she'd aim the bouquet in her mama's direction to encourage her to seek love again. But after Angelina turned her back to the ladies, the emcee told them to rearrange themselves.

On her way to the dance floor, Mama G stopped and recruited Mrs. Milanesi to join her. The older widow giggled like a schoolgirl and jumped on board immediately. Having his childhood caregiver from Lombardy here and being welcomed so readily by Angelina and her family as well as the D'Alessios this week was simply icing on the cake.

Speaking of which, he wanted to get this reception over so he could enjoy the first night of his married life.

"Ready, ladies?" the emcee asked.

Several of the women and girls shouted an exuberant *Yes!*, which had Angelina sending the bouquet flying. Carmella caught the flowers effortlessly, staring down wide-eyed at them as if she wasn't quite sure how they'd made it into her hands.

Everyone gathered around to congratulate her, and Megan snapped some photos of Carmella and Angelina, both spontaneous and posed ones. Afraid they might be whisked away without having a chance to convey their thanks, he pulled Megan aside when she was finished.

"I can't wait to see your photos, Megan," he said.

Joining him, Angelina added, "You've captured each important moment from our save-the-date to our engagement shoot to this moment and everything in between."

"Thank you for trusting me with these one-chance images. I'm excited to sit down with you two to work on your special albums and any prints you'll want to order. After you settle back in from your honeymoon, of course."

"How's Ryder?" Marc asked. He'd expected to see him at the church but knew there was no way he'd show up in a crowd this size.

"Thrilled that he was needed back at the ranch caring for a sick horse rather than having to be here." Megan shrugged with a crooked smile. "But he watched the wedding from the choir loft."

"I thought I saw someone up there," Angelina said, "but so much was going on as we left the altar that I wasn't sure."

"Thanks for understanding why he couldn't be here."

"No need to explain a thing to us," Marc said. PTSD had struck Ryder Wilson harder than the others who'd been on that rooftop in Iraq. "You know we would never push him. That he was present at the most meaningful part is all that matters."

"And you can bet we'll come out to the ranch whenever you've got the images ready. It'll be fun to spend some quiet time together with you two, and maybe Luke and Cassie can join us for dinner. I'll be back in the kitchen by then, too, so can provide the meal."

"Sounds wonderful," Megan said. "I'll never pass up one of your meals, Angelina."

Chapter Fourteen

"Okay, Marc, it's your turn," the emcee said, interrupting their conversation.

"If you'll excuse me, I think I'm needed for this part, too. My leg is, anyway." Angelina laughed as she walked to the center of the dance floor where a chair covered in an ivory satin skirt had been set.

"Your job is to remove Angelina's garter without touching it with anything but your teeth and lips."

The smoke in her eyes at those words set his heart to pounding. This might go a little beyond suggestive—not to mention embarrassing, considering they were surrounded by their mamas, Papa D., and her four brothers.

Game on.

She walked over to the chair, sat down, and let her attendants position the voluminous skirts to billow around her in a froth. However, no amount of tulle and lace would keep him from his goal.

Before he could make a move toward her, though, Rafe surprised him by taking a spot a few feet in front of her and crossing his arms over his chest as he stared Marc down. Her other brothers soon joined him.

Not another fistfight with Rafe. Hadn't they gotten that out of their systems last night?

"Oh, what's this? Looks like our groom is going to have to run a brotherly gauntlet to get to his bride's garter. Are you up to the challenge, Marc?" As master of ceremonies, he obviously took his job to keep the momentum going very seriously. Having the only microphone, perhaps he needed to.

"Oh, most definitely."

He wasn't sure if her brothers were pranking him or if they truly intended to make him break through their solid line. He'd do whatever it took, though, so they'd better be prepared.

"Don't hurt them, Marc!" Angelina shouted, giving him her vote of confidence. "I'm in no hurry!"

He turned toward her and said, "Well, as you know, *amore*, I am." He winked then regained his focus. After he took a couple of steps toward her brothers, they puffed themselves up while placing their hands at the ready on their hips.

"Hey, ladies, check out the impressive Giardano firefighters." The microphone amped up the announcement but didn't cover a couple whistles from the crowd.

He also heard a few ribald remarks and wondered if the brothers were somewhat embarrassed. But the wall of Giardanos didn't intimidate Marc in the least.

Angelina loved her brothers, so he had to be careful in how he set them straight—anything short of killing them ought to do. But if they thought he'd forgotten the intense Marine Corps training he underwent after he'd been assigned to Adam's unit as their Navy corpsman, they had better think again.

"An impressive sight," the emcee continued. "A solid line of Giardano firefighters—and they're all single, ladies!"

Marc was anything but impressed. Slowly, he advanced toward the Giardanos until he was toe-to-toe with Rafe. "I don't think your sister wants any blood on the dance floor tonight, so why don't you boys take your seats and let us continue?"

Unexpectedly, Rafe grinned. The bruise on his brother-in-law's cheek from last night's brawl made Rafe wince. Without any resistance, the brothers parted, two on either side. Marc must have passed some kind of test. His gaze fell on Angelina, who seemed as surprised as he was.

Without giving them an opportunity to change their minds, Marc went down on one knee, lifted the many hems of her dress, placed them in her lap, and grasped her calves as his hands slowly inched their way up her legs. Sparks shot into her eyes as he ignited a flame inside her that he hoped to keep alive for decades.

He lowered his head to her ankle and kissed her then blazed a trail of kisses and nibbles up her shapely leg. When he reached her knee, he lowered the gown over his head to the roaring approval of the crowd.

He thought he caught a glimpse of her bare mound, but surely she wouldn't go commando on her wedding day. Would she?

The garter was a few inches above her knee, but he wasn't ready to finish yet. He took a nip out of her thigh—just above the garter.

"Oh!" Angelina jumped, and the crowd laughed that he'd caught her by surprise. *Good.* He liked to keep her guessing.

"Looks like we have a biter," the emcee commented.

If you only knew what I wanted to bite right now.

He could smell her arousal, which only made him ache to get to their suite as soon as possible. The crowd began clapping rhythmically. Marc had better produce the lacy garter soon or her brothers might yank him out by his heels and drag him away. Taking the garter between his teeth, he slowly dragged it down her leg, releasing it to place another kiss at the side of her knee. Hearing her laughter made him harder than a boulder. It might be a good idea if he pulled her up to stand in front of him once he removed the garter.

Grabbing the satin with his teeth, he tugged it the rest of the way down her ankle until he reached her shoe. While not quite a stiletto, the three-inch heel posed a challenge. He stretched the elastic until he thought the garter would make it over the shoe, but lost his grip, leaving it dangling at her ankle. Biting down on the garter this time to make sure he didn't lose it again, he growled as he gave it a yank over her shoe. To everyone's laughter, he wound up taking her shoe with him. He picked up the shoe and placed it on her delicate foot, giving her a sheepish grin.

"Whew! I wasn't sure Marc was going to get the job done!" the emcee announced. Marc wasn't particularly thrilled with the guy's doubts about his abilities, but before he could respond, the man went on to say, "Okay, single gentlemen, gather on the dance floor. You're next!"

While they waited for the group of men to assemble, Angelina stood and closed the gap between them, placing a kiss on Marc's lips. "If I'd known a garter would get you so excited..." Obviously, she hadn't missed his boner. Fortunately, it was receding quickly. He'd save that for when he was alone with her in their suite tonight—which would be soon, he hoped.

"Come on! I know there are more single men in this room," the emcee cajoled.

Marc glanced over to see who had ventured onto the dance floor. Alessandro stood with his hands together, while Tony tried to coax his three brothers to join him. None looked like they had any intention of participating, but Mama G's plus one, Paul, was out there getting the side-eye from Rafe.

Damián gave Gunnar a good-natured nudge, and his mentor grinned with good humor before joining the small group that was rounded out by Sicilian and American cousins of various ages from both families and a server from Angelina's restaurant.

Not wanting to prolong the agony of the reluctant bachelors in the room or the semi-eager ones waiting on the dance floor, Marc gave a shout of "Heads up!" and pulled on the elastic garter. The scrap of material flew behind him. Before he could turn and see who the next groom might be, Angelina squealed, "Tony!"

It figured one of the Giardanos would catch the garter, even if only one of the four actually tried.

"Now, will the young lady who caught the bouquet join Tony on the dance floor?" the emcee asked. "We're going to have a little fun and do a reversal, letting Tony put the garter on your leg."

This should be interesting. The two had fought like cats and dogs during the wedding planning phase and had barely tolerated each other at rehearsal last night. Marc gathered Angelina in front of him, both of them facing Carmella who looked completely disgusted at the thought of having Tony's hands—or face—anywhere near her.

"Come on, Carm," Marc teased. "We won't hold you two to any official engagement or anything." As if *that* would ever happen.

Marc just wished they'd get on with it, because he couldn't wait to peel off every layer his bride wore when they got to their suite. At this rate, that was still hours away, so he'd better not let his mind stray too far again.

*   *   *

Angelina had never seen Tony so conflicted. He glanced down at the floor, then to the empty chair, and anywhere other than where Carmella stood rooted near the edge of the dance floor. What was the matter with him? Carmella, too, for that matter. It wasn't as if they'd been asked to strip down and have wild monkey sex or something.

"Tony, come on!" Angelina goaded. "Be a sport! You, too, Carmella, especially after you worked so hard on this reception."

As if her goading had given him some courage, Tony took a few steps toward Carmella and stretched out his hand. He'd placed the garter over his bicep for safekeeping, not expecting to lose it so soon, she supposed. Carmella still held the bouquet she'd caught minutes ago.

A blush crept up the young woman's neck and into her cheeks, no doubt from embarrassment. She preferred to hang in the background, from what Angelina could tell. But the longer she prolonged this, the more scrutiny she'd receive. With a sigh, she handed the bouquet to Cassie as she accepted Tony's proffered hand. He grinned as he guided her to the chair Angelina had just vacated.

Was it possible Carmella might have feelings for her brother? Her flushed cheeks could merely be from being in such a predicament, but if they stopped having to defend each other's families, might some attraction be allowed to grow between them? Angelina smiled. It would be something if her brother and Marc's sister became involved romantically.

Or was she just wrapped up in the afterglow of her own happily ever after tonight and letting her imagination run wild?

The wedding tradition merely stated that the woman who caught the bouquet and the man who caught the garter would be the next to marry—not that they'd marry each other. Still, Mama had told her that the couple who did so at her and Papa's wedding did actually marry each other, so perhaps…

"Same rules apply, Tony," Matteo yelled. "No hands on the garter!"

Carmella's tea-length bridesmaid skirt fell to her ankles when she sat down. Carmella's face grew redder, if possible, and she hiked the dress up above her knees. Maybe she didn't care for the idea of Tony's head being under her skirt. "Let's get this over with, T.G."

Angelina hadn't heard her refer to Tony as T.G. before.

"A little anticipation is good for you, *bella.*"

Tony had a nickname for her, too!

But Angelina's thoughts went straight to the Dom standing behind her who'd said that to her so many times. Apparently thinking the same thing, Marc chuckled, his hard chest reverberating against her back. Maybe all guys said stuff like that, though, because Tony didn't have a dominant bone in his body.

At least, not that *she'd* ever noticed.

"What's the matter? Afraid of something, T.G.?"

At Carmella's goading, Tony grinned and moved the garter down his sleeve to his wrist before kneeling in front of her. But instead of making any move to start the garter's path up her leg, he slipped off her sandal.

"Don't want your heel getting in my way, *principessa*." One hand cupped her calf gently while the other began massaging the ball of her foot. Carmella moaned.

Mio Dio, what's with all the endearments? These two were really getting into this. Had something been going on between them that Angelina had missed until now? They seemed to be awfully comfortable with each other, as if there weren't hundreds of people watching.

"Hurry up, T.G.," Carmella hissed under her breath.

Tony's grin widened as he placed the garter between his teeth and lowered his head to slip it past her toes. Above ankle level, he lowered her foot to the floor, but the garter slipped from his teeth. Securing the garter again, he made his way up to her calf before losing the garter again. Was he doing it on purpose? Tony wasn't a clumsy sort.

As if exasperated with him or wanting to put an end to her embarrassment, Carmella leaned forward as if to stand up.

"Sit," Tony commanded. "I'm not finished yet."

The command sent a little shiver down Angelina's spine. Surprisingly, Carmella settled back into the seat. Why was Angelina getting turned on watching her brother playing with Carmella and the garter? She was beginning to wish he'd hurry up, too. This reception couldn't be over soon enough. She wanted to be in Marc's arms—well, she already was. More specifically, she wanted him buried inside her, his body surrounding her...

Marc's thumb brushed the underside of her wrist, teasing her, as Tony took the garter between his teeth. Did Carmella spread her legs a little wider? He moved the elasticized lace a few inches

112

higher, pushing the hem of her skirt a little bit.

Marc lifted Angelina's hand to his lips and placed a kiss on her palm that sent another shiver down her spine. He whispered, "I don't know about you, but these two are giving me all kinds of ideas."

"I don't have a garter any longer, remember?"

"I'll improvise."

"Okay, T.G., that's far enough."

Their attention returned to the couple in front of them as Carmella took Tony by the shoulders and almost knocked him on his ass.

She stood and quickly rearranged her skirt to where the garter was now hidden. "Don't expect it back, either. I earned it."

Everyone laughed—except Tony. Angelina grinned at the perplexed look on his face. Carmella held out a hand to help him up, and after a long moment, Tony accepted then watched Carmella walk back to her table. He had the strangest expression on his face, as if he'd just been punched in the gut.

"Okay, what else do we have to do before we can get out of here?" Marc whispered in her ear, bringing her back to the present.

"I think that probably covers everything."

"Good. Now it's time for me to uncover that sexy body of yours."

Chapter Fifteen

M arc held Angelina's hand as they made their way up the grand staircase from the lobby to the honeymoon suite. He still wore his uniform and Angelina her dress, having just left the reception. But the moment he crossed that threshold, he'd finally get his hands on those buttons and reveal the luscious body the dress had hidden from him all day.

"I love Bella Montagna," Angelina said. "It's almost as if we're at a resort in the Dolomites."

"Would you like to go there someday?" He hadn't thought about a honeymoon in the mountains, because they lived on a mountain already. Would she be equally thrilled with the trip he *had* planned for them over the next ten days?

"I love to travel, especially with you, but with my restaurant and your career as an EMT—not to mention studying for your paramedic certification now—I think we'll have to put that off for a while. I'm just thrilled that we're going to have nine days before heading back to our crazy schedules."

They both loved what they did, despite how little time it left for them to be alone this past year, but their careers would settle down to a predictable routine eventually. Until then, they'd have to get creative at carving out more time for each other.

But the important thing was the quality of the time they did have together. Staying in the moment as they stole every precious minute together would be the key to wedded bliss.

At the second floor hallway, he retrieved the keycard from his jacket and led her to the door at the end of the hall. They'd enjoy this suite until leaving to catch their flight on Gunnar's jet out of Eagle tomorrow evening.

Marc opened the door but halted her when she started to walk through.

"Are you forgetting something?"

She furrowed her brow. "I thought you had our luggage brought up here already."

He shook his head with a grin then placed his arm under her thighs to swoop her into his embrace.

"Oh!" She regained her composure quickly and wrapped her arms around his neck. "How could I forget this part?"

Fortunately, he hadn't. This might not be the threshold of their new home—and he'd do it again there when they returned from their honeymoon—but he wouldn't start their marriage without performing the custom he knew began in ancient Rome.

He stepped into the living room of their suite with her adoring gaze on him. How'd he get to be such a lucky bastard? He placed a lingering kiss on her lips then released her legs so that her body slid slowly down his. His groin tightened in anticipation. Waiting for tonight had made this past week the longest of his life.

They'd had so much stress surrounding the wedding preparations this month that sex had been the furthest thing from their minds. He'd swapped two shifts with the two other EMTs at his station in order to have more time for their honeymoon. Both were happy to give Marc this time in exchange for them not having to work on Labor Day or Halloween, respectively.

Not to mention the fact that Marc and Angelina's house had been filled with out-of-town guests all week. The last time they'd tried to have sex this week, Angelina had been unable to achieve an orgasm, so he didn't force it. Their brief period of abstinence only made him want her more.

"Marc! Look at this place!" She spun around and took in one of the resort's most lavish suites. It was all he could do to tear his gaze away from her ass to see the room through her eyes as she wandered around the room checking everything out.

Ceiling beams led the eye to a bay window that took up most of the exterior wall. While she couldn't tell at night, he knew a stand of Colorado spruce trees blocked anyone from seeing into the room, so he'd instructed that the drapes remain open. A gas fire burned, adding warmth to the room, even though it was late June. He'd asked to have it lit when housekeeping came in for turn-down service because he intended for her to be naked posthaste and wouldn't want his new bride taking a chill.

Unless, of course, he chose to play with ice cubes again.

A bakery box sat on the coffee table next to a bowl of strawberries and a magnum of his favorite Trentodoc chilled in an ice bucket. Rather than another bottle of champagne, he'd had a little taste of Northern Italy sent from the wine cellar to their suite.

"I'll be right back." Angelina hurried from the room, hiking up her voluminous dress en route to the head. He crossed the room to pick up the bottle and peel away the foil.

When she reentered the room, she gravitated toward the heat of the fire. He almost wished Megan was here to capture a photo of her silhouetted against the fire with that sexy hairdo and her exquisite, curve-hugging gown before ridding her of both. Remembering his phone, he pulled it out and snapped a few pics of his unsuspecting bride. The images would help get him through those lonely nights away from her after he went back on duty.

Now, though, all he wanted was for her to be naked and for her hair to be in its natural state, long and flowing.

"We might not be in the Dolomites"—he popped the cork— "but we can certainly enjoy a wine made there." He half-filled the two goblets. "This bottle comes from Maso Martis vineyard's 2011 vintage, significant because some of the grapes that went into making this wine were harvested the same month that I met you."

She smiled. "Oh, Marc. You are incredibly romantic, and I love you for it." She closed the gap between them and placed a kiss on his cheek before accepting a half-filled goblet of the sparkling rosé.

He lifted his to her. "To a lifetime of love—and hot, passionate sex."

"Hear, hear!" Angelina giggled as they clinked glasses, and each took a sip. She closed her eyes and moaned as the smooth flavors filled her mouth. *Merda*, he wanted to fill that mouth, too. His cock hardened, but he'd control himself long enough to let her finish at least one glass of the expensive wine while he decided where he wanted to start. There was no end to the number of ways he intended to enjoy his voluptuous bride's body tonight.

He tossed back the rest of his wine.

* * *

The sparkling wine tickled all the way down her throat. She hadn't really had much to drink at the reception and didn't want to get more than a slight buzz tonight, because she was ready to strip that sexy sailor out of his uniform. She, too, guzzled the rest of hers, and both set their glasses down on the table.

The strawberries looked delicious, and she guessed that box contained the cake he'd asked be sent here. Would he exact revenge on her for smashing that slice of cake into his face at the reception? Or would he let her enjoy it by smearing some on her breasts and licking it off, like he did the day of the cake tasting?

She loosened his bowtie, never taking her eyes off him, but he captured her hands before she could start unbuttoning his shirt. She surrendered to his smoldering gaze, recognizing the instant when his Dom came out to play. Marc had been hinting since last night's rehearsal dinner that he definitely wanted to play tonight, and after their stress-filled week—her preparing for the wedding and Marc working insane hours—they were both more than ready.

"Turn around."

Angelina didn't hesitate to follow his command. His lips grazed the side of her neck as he brushed his knuckles down the exposed part of her back.

"I love this dress on you, especially this open back." His tongue licked down her spine before reaching the fabric of the dress again. "But these buttons have been on my mind since the moment I saw them. I'm looking forward to seeing you out of the dress even more."

"Please, Sir, even though they've been uncomfortable to sit on, be gentle with the buttons. Our daughter might one day want to wear this dress." She could just picture him ripping it at the seams for quicker access. He merely chuckled, which didn't tell her what he had in mind at all.

"Interlock your hands behind your head."

He usually saved this pose for when she was already naked and he wanted to lift her girls, but it wasn't for her to question why. She placed her hands over her updo, laced her fingers, and waited.

Moments later, his hands brushed the curve of the fabric covering her ass. Would he be surprised at what he was about to discover? No doubt, but he would also be pleased. And pleasing this man was utmost on her list of priorities.

Marc undid the hook holding the top of the dress together, then immediately began unbuttoning the cloth-covered buttons over her ass. His warm hands occasionally skimmed the bare skin on her back, and he'd probably only gotten to the fourth or fifth button when he muttered, "*Merda.*"

She grinned. "Is everything all right, Sir?" A shiver of raw sexuality coursed through her.

"So you really wore no panties to the altar?"

"I won't tell Father Bancroft if you won't, Sir."

"*Gesù*, woman! It's probably best I didn't know, or I might have messed up your dress beyond repair in the limo ride to the reception."

She giggled, but it died when his tongue licked down the crease of her ass. Drawing in a sharp breath, she waited. Instead of continuing to undo her buttons, he stood and pressed himself against her back, his hands cupping her breasts.

"This dress has got to go, one way or another," he whispered in her ear. "Help me, or it might be in shreds in the next few seconds."

Angelina lowered her arms in an instant, and while Marc undid a few more buttons, she tugged the sleeves down her arms until the bodice fell forward and bared her breasts. Although he couldn't see them, his hands zeroed in immediately on her nipples, pinching and twisting them until she creamed a little more. She bit her lower lip to keep from losing her composure, although he hadn't told her she needed to be stoic.

Marc's thumbs hooked the dress at her hips and he pushed it down until it pooled at her feet. She started to bend down to pick it up, but a slap on her butt cheek stilled her. "Help me undress."

She turned, and his red-hot gaze pierced hers before shifting his focus to her breasts. "Gorgeous, woman. The most gorgeous woman in the world, and you're mine."

She blushed at his words but went to work slipping off his coat and placing it carefully onto the sofa before unbuttoning his shirt and baring that mouthwatering chest. She wanted to run her fingers through the tufts of hair at the center, but her instructions were to get him out of his uniform, so that was her primary focus.

She undid the belt and buttons, and his rigid cock sprang out. "I see I'm not the only one who went commando today."

"Angelina…" His warning tone told her she had a job to do, and she pushed the pants down his legs before remembering he still wore his shoes and socks.

"Lift your left foot, Sir." He did so, and she untied and slipped off the shoe then his sock before asking him to lift the other one and doing the same. His cock was so close to her mouth she could taste it. Maybe he wouldn't mind if she took a quick lick. Her tongue darted out to flick against the underside of his hard rod. His sharp intake of air told her she'd hit the spot, but he was soon hauling her up by her hair.

"Not so fast. If anyone's getting a first taste, it's going be me. I can smell your arousal."

"Perhaps you should kick those pants off, and we can head to the bedroom."

"Who's calling the shots, *amore?*"

"You are, Sir."

"That's right. Now, present that pretty little ass for me. Bend over the arm of that sofa, and spread your legs."

She nearly came at his words but managed to take up the position he'd ordered her into while he finished undressing. Would she be punished for not completing her task before getting completely sidetracked? The thought of a spanking made her even hotter. When the leather of his belt cracked over her ass, she moaned. *Don't stop, Sir. Please!*

Several additional blows fell before he tossed the belt onto the sofa in front of her face. "That ought to teach you not to disobey me again."

"Yes, Sir." She knew he'd merely found the slightest excuse for an infraction so he could give her what she craved more than anything except that rock-hard cock he was about ram into her pussy. *Mio Dio*, was she ever wet and ready.

But instead of his cock, she got his tongue, teeth, and lips. He nipped at her pussy lips, making her spread her legs a little wider to give him better access to her molten core. He avoided her clit, which ached with need, and lapped up her juices like a man in the desert. He rammed his fingers inside her—it must have been three at once. Time for her to spring her second surprise on him.

"Sir, there's something you should know."

He pulled away from her. "Are you in any pain? You have your safewords."

"No, it's not that. I feel divine. I just wanted to tell you that...well"—why was she hemming and hawing?—"this week, I've been wearing my plugs." That was as close as she intended to get to asking him to fuck her up the ass on her wedding night.

* * *

Gesù, *take me now.*

Marc had hoped to pleasure her first, although clearly the woman was as fond of anal as he was, but hearing her words had him close to shooting his load down her legs and not where it counted.

"Do. Not. Move."

He hurried into the bedroom, where earlier he'd left his toy bag, and pulled out some lube and a condom. Might as well do this now then shower before continuing this marathon night of lovemaking with his bride. He rolled on the condom and squirted the lube on his cock before returning to the living room where her glorious ass was exposed and waiting for him. He liberally coated her puckered star with lube as well and stroked her clit to make sure she was as close to exploding as he was.

"Oh, yesss!" Her hips bucked as she moaned.

They hadn't had anal for months, though, so he needed to be gentle. "What size plugs did you use?"

"I inserted the biggest one two days ago. Even wore it to daVinci's."

Fuck!

Unable to wait a moment longer, he pressed his cock's head against her opening. "Bear down." She pushed back against him and took him in with a plop. *Merda!* He tried to pull out before plowing into her a little harder, but her ass gripped him and wouldn't let go. "You're going to be the death of me, woman."

"Don't you dare die on me yet, husband! Now, fuck me!"

He didn't even care that she'd just topped him but gave her a perfunctory swat to the ass cheek anyway. Her sphincter muscle squeezed him even harder, and he rammed his way home. After a moment, he pulled back and rammed her again.

"Yes! Like that, Sir! Harder!"

Angelina would always be a brat, always topping from the bottom. But he didn't care at the moment. They developed a rhythm he knew wouldn't last long. "Here comes the bride," he predicted, hoping she'd beat him to the climax.

A brief giggle escaped her until he flicked his finger against her swollen clit. Her eyes widened as she screamed, "I'm coming! Ohh! Yesss!"

With a long, drawn-out grunt, Marc came as the two climaxed together. He draped his body over her back, not wanting to break this intimate contact as he gasped for air. "Fucking intense, and totally *not* what I had planned for you tonight. Tomorrow, maybe, but not the first time."

"You won't hear any complaints from me, Sir. I've missed butt sex."

While it had only been a couple of months, apparently he needed to step up his game. "Remind me not to neglect my wife's needs again for the next, oh, seventy years or so. And I thank you for having the foresight to prepare yourself, despite all you've had on your plate."

Marc stood, eased himself out of her, and discarded the condom. When he returned to the sofa where she'd maintained her position perfectly—whether because she was being a good submissive or was too exhausted to move, he wasn't sure—he helped her to her feet.

Angelina melted against him, wrapping her arms around his waist as she caressed the curve of his ass. "My legs are as limp as overcooked pasta."

Giving her time to regain her equilibrium, he began removing flowers and hairpins from her carefully coifed hair. He wanted that glorious mane loose and free. But it didn't seem to budge much at all.

"How much hairspray did they use on you?"

"More than I wanted, but she insisted I needed it to keep everything in place throughout the day."

Time to take care of that and some other things. He lifted his bride once again and carried her through the living room and over the threshold of the bedroom they would spend their first married night in. But he didn't stop, instead going directly into the bathroom. "Soak or shower?"

"Shower, if you're going to join me."

"Perfect answer, pet."

They spent ten minutes washing each other thoroughly and removing the hairspray from her do, until Angelina grasped his erection. "Permission to worship my husband's cock, Sir?"

His penis jolted in her hand, giving her his body's unequivocal response. He hadn't expected to be ready again so soon. She waited for verbal permission, seeming to remember her training again. Even though they were mostly a role-playing D/s couple, she did enjoy being a service submissive, which also brought him a lot of pleasure.

"I'd love nothing more than to have my wife's hot mouth on my cock right now." Whoever said sex after marriage wasn't nearly as exciting as before clearly wasn't married to a woman like Angelina.

Rather than have her kneel on the tiles, he positioned her in front of the granite seat in the corner and indicated she should sit. "Suck my cock, wife."

"Yes, Sir." She smiled up at him and didn't let her eyes stray from his as she took him deep into her hot mouth until he bumped the back of her throat.

Expecting her to pull away, she shocked him by taking the head of his cock into her throat and swallowing around him. The muscles contracted around him, squeezing him tighter than a fist.

"*Gesù!*"

Not wanting to hurt her, he grabbed onto her head to push her away, but she grunted, the vibration also felt to his core. Once again, she surprised him as she inched him farther down her throat. She'd always enjoyed giving him blow jobs but never like this. Had she been practicing deep throating?

"That feels amazing, *amore.*"

Her eyes twinkled—or were they tears? Just a moment longer, and he'd insist that she stop. But Angelina didn't seem to want to put an end to this any more than he did. Instead, she reached for his balls and began massaging them.

"If you don't want my cum down your throat, *bella*, you might tread lightly there."

She continued to stroke his balls, which were now against her chin, so that each time she moved her mouth, she stimulated him from both sides.

"I'm close to the point of no return!"

She took him a little deeper, and he exploded. "*Merda!* You're incredible!" His cum spilled down her throat until he eased her off his pulsating shaft. His hypersensitive cock continued to twitch as he pulled out ever so slowly.

Angelina smiled up at him. "I hope you enjoyed my wedding present to you."

"Enjoyed is putting it lightly. How'd you learn to do that?" Skill like that came from more than watching videos.

"With a small silicone dildo. I've been practicing for months to get beyond my gag reflex."

Marc helped her to her feet. "I think you succeeded." He kissed her, his tongue exploring the mouth where his cock had been a minute ago. When he pulled away, he brushed the wet hair away from her face. "But no more practicing without me."

"That dildo was nothing compared to the amazing feeling of

you in my throat." She kissed him lightly. "I might need to rest my throat before the next time, though. *Dio*, that was intense!"

"I assure you, I'll be ready anytime you are. Now, let's dry off and go to bed so I can get my tongue on your clit."

Her sharp intake of breath sounded like she hadn't expected more, but Marc would spend the rest of his life pleasing this woman who had brought so much peace and joy to his life.

Chapter Sixteen

The plane touched down in Milan the next day, and Marc stood to help Mrs. Milanesi up. Angelina couldn't wait to get off Gunnar's jet and begin exploring Marc's homeland again, but when she began gathering her belongings, he stayed her hand.

"Relax here, *cara*. I'll be back for you momentarily."

She grinned. Did he plan on making love on the plane again? Might be a little awkward with Gunnar and Patrick onboard, but that didn't stop them last year.

"Mrs. Milanesi, you take good care of yourself. Thank you so much for making your way to Colorado for our wedding."

"I wouldn't have missed it for the world." In her Northern Italian dialect, she said to Marc as she cupped his chin, "*Bambino mio*, you take good care of your angel. She's the only one for you."

"Don't I know it. I'll take excellent care of her."

The old woman then addressed them both. "And thank you for allowing me the experience of my first private jet flight. I didn't mean to intrude on your honeymoon."

"Nonsense," Angelina argued. "It's been a delight to hear more stories about my husband's boyhood years." She winked at Marc before continuing. "My first private jet ride was last year when we came to see you." She remembered fondly Marc's effort to win her back taking her along on the trip—not just for the romantic elements but to show he could make her a part of his journey to find answers from his past. Man, had he ever succeeded, because she'd said yes to his proposal on the flight home.

After she hugged and kissed the woman goodbye, Marc disembarked with his childhood caregiver to reunite her with her son-in-law. She wasn't sure why he didn't have her start through customs rather than wait here. Without Italian citizenship, it would take her longer, but she'd use the opportunity to ground herself.

Placing a set of noise canceling headphones over her ears to listen to Bocelli's melodic voice, she sat back, closed her eyes, and relaxed against the leather seat. Would he take her to dinner at the same place as last year? If so, she couldn't wait to try something new on the menu.

A hand stroked her upper arm, and she nearly jumped out of the seat. She opened her eyes to find Marc grinning down at her. Removing the headphones, she said, "I must have dozed off."

"I'm sorry if I woke you but wanted to tell you to buckle up before we take off again."

"You mean, this isn't our honeymoon destination?"

"No, *amore*."

He'd been secretive about their honeymoon destination, but when he'd offered Mrs. Milanesi a ride, she'd simply assumed it would be in the area of his birth. Asking wouldn't elicit any response, so she buckled her seatbelt with anticipation as Marc took his seat across from her.

At their cruising altitude, now that they were alone, he guided her to the U-shaped sofa and cradled her in his arms.

The jolt when they landed jarred her awake. She glanced out the windows, but it looked like any other airport.

After taking Gunnar and Patrick aside to thank them for the wedding gift of allowing them to be passengers on Gunnar's jet and make arrangements for their rendezvous flight, Marc led Angelina down the stairs to the tarmac. At customs, the agent said, "Welcome to Catania. Is this your first visit here?"

Without replying to the agent, Angelina turned and threw herself into Marc's arms. "Thank you, thank you, thank you. I mean

Grazie, grazie, grazie. Marc, I never dreamed you'd bring me back to Sicily for our honeymoon. I haven't been here since I lost my *nonna*."

"I've always wanted to see Sicily, so I did have ulterior motives."

"I thought you might bring me back to Italy, given the length of time the flight took, but I assumed we'd go to Lombardy or Tuscany again."

"Last year, I showed you some of the significant places from my childhood. Now you can show me the places you saw so often during visits to your *nonna*."

"I can't wait!"

Forty minutes later, she settled into the front seat of the sporty convertible Marc had rented. She rested her head against the leather and breathed in the salty air. Memories from childhood wafted through her mind.

"Where are we staying?"

"You'll see."

Ahead of them, Mount Etna towered above the landscape with an expanse of thousands of buildings stretching out to the foot of the peak. When she thought he'd veer off toward the west, he kept driving closer and closer to the volcano. Was he taking her to see the volcano?

"I never got this close to it as a kid." Nonna lived in Marsala on the opposite end of the island and hadn't been able to drive, so they'd pretty much stayed in that part of Sicily during her visits.

"Seriously?"

She shook her head then realized his gaze was on the road and said, "Nope."

He stopped the car at an overlook, and she took it all in. The terra-cotta roofs were so familiar.

"How'd you like to spend the night on Etna?"

"How close?"

He chuckled. "Well, the hotel had to be rebuilt after the 1983 eruption and now sits on a lava bed."

Her heartbeat ramped up. While Marc would always be the adventurous one, she was a little excited about being in such close proximity to such a powerful, volatile force of nature.

Oh, and being close to Mount Etna was a thrill, too.

Spontaneously, she unbuckled her seatbelt and launched herself at him, being careful not to move the stick shift. He quickly adjusted his seat away from the steering wheel to accommodate her in his lap.

"Marc, it's amazing! I can't believe we're here."

"Well, we aren't there yet." His fingers pushed the hair away from her cheeks, and he pulled her closer for a kiss. His hand lowered to cup her breast and pinch her nipple before he took her by the shoulders and set her back in her seat with a sigh. "If we sit here much longer, I'm going to have you straddling my hips with my cock buried deep inside your pussy."

Her breath caught in her throat. "What if that's what I want right now?"

He tapped her nose. "I'd tell you anticipation is good for you." No surprise there. He often told her that. "Besides, we have dinner reservations tonight. Buckle up again, and let's go."

"Yes, Sir!" Marc hadn't been this Dom-like in months. She couldn't wait to have him all to herself for the remainder of this honeymoon. Well, *mostly* to herself. She did have a lot of relatives on the island. Unless he chose not to tell anyone they were here. They *were* on their honeymoon, after all. Her family would understand if they kept to themselves, assuming they even knew they were in Sicily.

Back in her seat, she took in the fast-moving scenery as they sped through the streets of Catania on their way to Mount Etna. Angelina wanted to pinch herself to see if this was real.

"Your cousins told me at the wedding that we'd have to pay a visit to Marsala to see the family members who didn't make it to the States last week, especially your great uncles and aunts."

She leaned over and kissed him on the cheek. "Thank you so much for that!" Would she recognize Nonna's house? If not, her relatives would be able to point it out to her.

"But we're staying on this side of the island the first few days." He pointed toward the volcano. "Want to take a tour of the crater tomorrow?"

"You don't think it will have an eruption while we're here, do you?"

He gave a shrug. "There were some fireworks in March, but she's been quiet since then. Still, it's exciting to spend our first two nights on the volcano."

Always the thrill seeker. A sudden thought made her heart jump into her throat. "Please tell me we aren't camping on our honeymoon."

His laugh was long and hearty. "No, my lovely bride. I know your hard limits. We might camp out on a beach in Taormina in a few days, but for the next two nights, we're staying in a modern hotel."

"Still, being so close to Etna will be a thrilling adventure. As long as there's a bed, a bathroom, and my sexy husband, I'm good to go!"

*   *   *

Marc had been planning this trip for six months, and the Hotel Corsaro didn't disappoint. Not as luxurious as his family's Bella Montagna by any stretch, the view of Mount Etna outside their window made up for it.

As he guided her out for a stroll in the gardens, the scents of floral herbs and the Mediterranean evening surrounded them. "I can't believe I'm in Sicily—with you," she said, looking up at him with a smile. "Thank you so much. You've made me happy beyond words."

He stopped and took her into his arms as he stared into her face. "And I'll be happy wherever I am, as long as you're with me."

Tomorrow, they would hike the forest and go up to the crater on a tour, but after the long flight, all he wanted to do was take his wife to bed. After enjoying some exquisite Sicilian meals, of course.

They had dinner reservations in an hour at *Rifugio Sapienza*, and their seafood had come highly recommended. Thank goodness it was only a few miles away, though, because Marc couldn't wait any longer to touch his wife.

He lifted Angelina's hair from her neck and placed a kiss there then another near her collarbone. Her pulse pounded against his lips. They'd certainly made love numerous times in the honeymoon suite on their wedding night and the next morning—and enjoyed a much-needed spanking to get her mind off what was happening at her restaurant—but he'd barely touched her since then. She'd been going nonstop for a week to prepare for the wedding, and he had wanted her to catch up on her sleep during the flight.

He cupped her breast and squeezed before pinching her nipple. Her moan told him all he needed to know. Scooping her into his arms, he carried her to the bed where he placed her on her feet. Standing behind her, he began removing her clothing, which hindered his being able to take her at the moment.

"I can undress myself, sweetheart." She reached for the hem of her blouse, but he stilled her hands.

"It's more fun when I do it."

Angelina raised her hands. "I won't argue with you there. But hurry. You said we have dinner reservations."

He swatted her ass. "Who's in charge in our bedroom—wherever that bedroom may be?"

"You—*most* of the time."

"Brat."

She giggled, but when she tried to dance away from him, Marc yanked the blouse over her head to prove he'd be calling the shots. He tossed it on a nearby chair before wrapping his arms around her to fiddle with the bra clasp between her breasts. He could have released it in a second but took his time, pinching her nipples between his knuckles while playfully fumbling around.

"Need help?"

He growled.

"Sorry, Sir." She leaned back against him as if to let him have his fun. A few moments later, he spread the scraps of material open and turned her to face him. Bending, he took one swollen nipple into his mouth. She grabbed the back of his head with both hands as if to hold him captive. Later tonight, he'd definitely be making use of the restraints he'd packed. No time for that now.

Latching onto her nipple with his teeth, he pulled away until she squealed in pain to remind her who was in control. He released the swollen peak, grinning as her breast bounced back into a resting position—for the time being. "Remove your shoes then interlock your hands behind your head."

Angelina complied while he positioned some pillows on the bed. He knelt down in front of her to draw her slacks down her legs, and she stepped out of them. He left on the panties for now. She wouldn't be wearing them the rest of the night, so he'd enjoy their sexiness a little while.

With his hands on her ass, he pulled her crotch to his face and inhaled her essence. She stiffened, no doubt worried that she hadn't showered since they'd left the Eagle airport, but to her credit, she didn't tell him to stop. She still had her hang-ups about certain things he enjoyed the hell out of. But he'd been thinking about eating her pussy all the way across the Atlantic, so nothing short of a safeword would stop him.

That's probably all he'd have time to do to her before dinner anyway. He'd have her screaming his name, along with a few choice curse words, multiple times within the next half hour, with no thoughts in her head about anything but reaching her first climax. *Merda*, he so loved to tease and torment her.

Releasing his hold, he sat back on his heels. "Remove your panties and lie on your back with your ass on the pillows."

"Yes, Sir." She shimmied out of her panties, and he enjoyed the view of her bare mound and flashes of her pussy lips as she assumed the position.

It took every ounce of effort to keep from diving right in, but instead, he began nipping at the insides of her knees, slowly blazing a trail upward. When she could barely lie still on the bed, he ceased his kisses until her squirming stopped.

Locking his arms around her thighs, he simply stared at her already wet pussy a few moments. He'd never tire of the sight. He lowered his face until his tongue slid the length of her cleft. *Sweet as honey.* His thumbs pulled her lips apart, and he blew on her clit until she squirmed, but she remembered her discipline and didn't hurry him along.

Without warning, he flicked his tongue back and forth on her clit, and she gasped and tensed before pressing her pussy against him again. Removing his right hand from around her thigh, he dipped his middle finger inside her then quickly added a second finger. So wet for him. His cock strained against his zipper. He plunged in and out as his tongue flicked in ever-increasing movements against her clit.

"Sir, permission to come!"

Aw, fuck. He wasn't sure he'd be able to sit at the dinner table with her tonight knowing how hot and wet she was for him if he didn't get more than a taste right now. Maybe there was time for a quickie and both of them could get some relief. Standing, he undid his pants and removed them, her gaze alternating between his cock and his face. Her smile told him she wanted him deep inside her, too.

Chapter Seventeen

*C*ome on! Don't keep me waiting!

Marc's infuriating smile had her close to shouting those words, but she fought for what little control she could muster. After an interminable wait, he rested his upper body on one arm while positioning his cock against her opening. It wouldn't take much more friction against her clit for her to explode.

Hurry, Marc! I need this!

She'd been insatiable since their wedding night. He teased his cock between her soaking wet opening and equally wet clit. *So close.*

Marc lowered himself over her body, resting on both forearms now. "Look at me." She met his gaze seconds before he plowed into her pussy to the hilt. Her eyes opened wide, and she had to fight the urge to close them without permission but still managed to savor the moment of intense fullness before he pulled almost completely out of her. "I love watching you take me."

"And I love being taken by you." *Now, get it in gear, sailor. I need to come!*

She tilted her hips slightly to invite him back in, and he buried himself again then withdrew. Why was he taking so long to get to the pace she needed to climax?

"Is my bride impatient with her groom?"

Direct question. "Hell, yes!"

"Are you ready?"

"More than."

"You do not have permission to come until I tell you."

And with that, he began to piston her so hard her clit was stimulated with each thrust. He lowered his mouth to first one nipple, which he sucked and nipped, and then the other. Stimulation on three fronts was almost more than she could take, and her entire body shook with her effort to hold back the orgasm wanting to tear through her.

"Marc, please! I need to come."

He released her nipple and smiled down at her, his hips never slowing down. She gritted her teeth as a sheen of sweat broke out on her forehead. She grasped the sheets and fought to hold on. Then he slipped his hand between their bodies and stroked her clit.

"*Mio Dio!*" She wasn't going to be able to withstand this latest barrage of sensations.

"Come for me, *amore*."

Thank you, Gesù! And Marc, too. The earth shook as she exploded under him. Was Mount Etna erupting or was that merely her world? Marc pounded into her a few more times as the peak of her climax ebbed and shouted, "Yes! Christ, you're so tight and hot around my cock."

Watching his face as he let go sent a surge of emotions through her. No more masks. They'd been long gone. She'd never tire of seeing Marc in his most elemental state.

Marc rolled off her and onto his back, staring up at the ceiling. His chest rose and fell rapidly at first. "Woman, you're going to be my undoing."

She propped herself on her hand and ran her finger down the center of his chest. "What on earth do you mean?"

"When I'm with you, all I want to do is have sex. But I will have to function in other ways eventually."

"You can worry about other things after the honeymoon. Right now, all we have to think about is pleasing ourselves—and having sex with you always pleases me."

"Me, too!"

Marc had told her Gunnar would be gone seven or eight days on his humanitarian mission to Afghanistan, but he was scheduled to work on the Fourth of July. They'd have plenty of time for at least a hundred orgasms!

"How dressy do we need to be for dinner?" she asked.

"A summer dress would be perfect—but no panties for the rest of this honeymoon."

"Seriously? But I bought some new thongs just for you."

He growled before saying, "I might let you wear a thong in the bedroom, but I want that pretty ass of mine bare and ready for anything, anytime.

"As you wish, my husband."

Her stomach knotted, whether from the smoldering Dom stare or her hunger, she wasn't sure. She intended to be in a constant state of arousal, both for Marc and for the amazing food she'd consume here.

And his choice of *ristorante* tonight did not disappoint. They took their time dining over three hours at the world-renowned *Rifugio Sapienza* while he shared some of the things he planned for them to do in Sicily. Each course was a delight, but she struggled to name some of the elusive ingredients used. From seafood to pasta to a mouthwatering chocolate cake, it was all she could do not to ask to visit the chef in the kitchen when, to her surprise, he showed up at their table to check on them.

In Sicilian dialect, she raved about every dish and even coaxed the man into a tour of his kitchen anytime she wanted during her visit. Knowing that would bore Marc, she didn't want to go back there now, although it was hard to watch the chef walk away without her.

Angelina suggested they order two glasses of *elisir dei sette potenti* and two coffees for after dinner. She hadn't enjoyed the fiery liqueur exploding in her mouth since Nonna let her try it on one of her last visits to Sicily.

"*Merda!* That packs some heat."

She laughed, already feeling more laid back. "It roughly translates to 'elixir of the seven powers,' but that estimate might be on the low side."

As the beverage burned a path to her stomach, she became more languid. She hadn't had this much to drink in a long time but didn't feel intoxicated. Just...mellow.

Marc asked for the check.

Angelina groaned, her hand on her belly. "I might have to pace myself—on both food and drink. Perhaps we should eat earlier in the day tomorrow and work off some of the food by taking a hike," she suggested. "I want you proud to be seen with me despite all the weight I'll gain here."

He gently tilted her face to look into her eyes and stroked her cheek before leaning in for a smoldering kiss. If she wasn't drunk on wine and liqueur, she'd be drunk on love.

Pulling away, he said, "Let me assure you, nothing would ever make me reluctant to show you off or to be seen with you. You're the sexiest woman alive, Angelina. That you chose to make me your husband makes me feel like a king."

Her face flushed. "Well, you'll always be the 'King of Love' to me." Her mind replayed that tune from the Mary Chapin Carpenter CD she'd had on her stereo the night Marc and Luke had come over for dinner at her place. Seemed like forever ago.

He settled the check then stood and pulled out her chair.

Angelina became aware of her bare pussy lips the moment they stepped out of the restaurant into the cool evening air when a stiff breeze lifted the hem of her dress. She managed to hold it down, front and back, to avoid giving a show to any patrons in the parking lot. She wasn't sure she'd succeeded after two men smiled her way as they walked to the convertible.

Marc's arm around her back and waist helped her navigate the uneven pavement. As he reached for the door, he said with a grin,

"I think my wife is ready for bed."

"More than ready, Sir. And wet. Ssooo wet for her husband."

A fire burned in his eyes that matched the one in her belly that seemed to have moved farther down now. "I've been waiting to get my hands on that ass again since we left the hotel."

*   *   *

On Monday evening, bringing their last full day in Sicily to a satisfying end, Marc and Angelina sat surrounded by her large extended family at her great-uncle's home in Marsala. The warm, salt breeze wafted, and notes of lemon and rosemary permeated the air. Angelina hadn't been here since Nonna died, but these scents evoked strong memories for her. She could almost feel Nonna's presence, just as she had at her wedding, only here it was quite a bit stronger.

Marc nuzzled her neck, well into his third—or perhaps fourth—glass of wine. They'd been celebrating their marriage with extended family members for hours, with no end in sight. They hadn't even seen the *dolce* course yet. Was Marc impatient to have her alone again in their room? They had a third of the house to themselves, even with the addition of Gunnar and Patrick staying overnight before the return flight home tomorrow. Uncle Vincenzo's house was more luxurious than any of the hotels they'd stayed at. To say her Sicilian family had done well in the olive oil business was an understatement.

Angelina was excited about the case of last season's family reserve stock her great-uncle had gifted her with to take home to her restaurant. Two more cases would follow every October from the current year's first cold-pressing. She'd make it last all year, only using it as a finishing oil in salads and on dishes after cooking. She couldn't wait to share the oil with diners at her restaurant. There was no comparison between what she could buy in the States and what her family grew here in Marsala.

"To our American family not taking so long to visit next time!" her second cousin Lorenzo said, grinning as he raised his glass. "Their friends are always welcome, too!" he added with a nod toward Gunnar and Patrick.

Everyone seated at the massive table under the vine-covered pergola lifted their glass and took another drink. Toasts had abounded throughout the meal, and she felt more than a little buzzed. Good thing they didn't have to drive anywhere, but she would like to make it back to their room under her own steam.

Not that she would trade this evening for anything. Reminiscing about Nonna and so many other ancestors who'd lived on this land for centuries taught her even more about her roots. Not wanting this magical moment to end, she leaned her head against Marc's shoulder. Just as he had done in Lombardy last year, she'd been able to share her family's heritage with him and looked forward to bringing their children here someday to soak up their culture, as her parents had done with her and her brothers in their formative years. The boys hadn't spent time with her and Nonna in the kitchen those summers. Instead, they'd enjoyed going fishing and running around the olive groves and Marsala with their male cousins.

"What are you thinking about, *amore*?"

The sound of the mandolin one of her young cousins played filtered into her thoughts as she thought about how to answer him. "Many things, but mostly about my family and how much I love them." She sat upright and faced him, smiling. "And how happy I am you're a part of my family now and how much fun it will be expanding *our* family and growing old together."

"That's a lot more thinking than my wine-mellowed brain can attempt tonight." His eyes smoldered as he leaned in to kiss her. She tuned out the cheers around them as he deepened the kiss, hoping they would be able to escape to their room soon. In Italy, public displays of affection weren't looked down upon as they might be at home. Her cheeks burned with desire rather than embarrassment.

When she pulled away, he smiled. "Italy has only made your passions run deeper and hotter, *bella*."

"We are going to keep loving at this intensity for the rest of our lives."

"Count on me to be ready and willing anytime you're interested, even a hundred years from now."

"Wow, a true Italian stallion, huh?"

He cupped the side of her face and leaned closer. "*Your* Italian stallion—and I won't let you forget that as long as we live, Mrs. Angelina D'Alessio."

*For timely updates and much more, sign up for her e-mails or text alerts on her website at **kallypsomasters.com**.*

Books by Kallypso Masters

Rescue Me Saga (Erotic Romance)

Kally has no intention of ending the *Rescue Me Saga* ever, but will introduce some new series with new characters in the years to come. The following *Rescue Me Saga* titles are available in e-book and print formats on my web site and at major booksellers:

Masters at Arms & Nobody's Angel (Combined Volume)
Nobody's Hero
Nobody's Perfect
Somebody's Angel
Nobody's Lost
Nobody's Dream
Somebody's Perfect

Rescue Me Saga Box Set Books 1-3 (always e-book only)
Rescue Me Saga Box Set Books 4-6 and Western Dreams (always e-book only)

Rescue Me Saga Extras (Erotic Romance)

This will be a series of hot, fun, short-story collections featuring beloved couples from the *Rescue Me Saga*.

Western Dreams (Rescue Me Saga Extras #1)
Wedding Dreams (Rescue Me Saga Extras #2)

Raging Fire Series (Steamy Romance Serials)

A series of four serialized novels being published initially on Kally's Patreon page that features Angelina Giardano's four firefighter brothers. First, enjoy *Tony: Slow Burn* **(Raging Fire #1)** which will be followed by Matteo's, Franco's, and Rafe's stories. After serialization is finished, the stories will be edited and published as e-books and available wherever you buy books.

Roar
(a *Rescue Me Saga* Erotic Romance Spin-off)

(Erotic Romance with Secondary Characters from the *Rescue Me Saga. Roar* provides a lead into the upcoming trilogy with Patrick, Grant, and Gunnar's stories. No clue when that series will be written. Kally is waiting for Grant to open up.)

Bluegrass Spirits (Supernatural Contemporary Romance)

(Contemporary Romance…with a Haunting Twist)

Jesse's Hideout

Kate's Secret

kallypsomasters.com/books

About the Author

Kallypso Masters is a *USA Today* Bestselling Author with more than half-a-million copies of her books sold in e-book and paperback formats since August 2011. All her books feature alpha males, strong women, and happy endings because those are her favorite stories to read, but that doesn't mean they don't touch on the tough issues sometimes. Her best-known series—the Rescue Me Saga—features emotional, realistic adult Romance novels with characters healing from past traumas and PTSD, sometimes using unconventional methods (like BDSM).

An eighth-generation Kentuckian, in spring 2017, Kally launched the new ***Bluegrass Spirits*** series, supernatural Contemporary Romances set in some of her favorite places in her home state. *Jesse's Hideout* (Bluegrass Spirits #1) is set in her father's hometown in Nelson County and includes a recipe section with some of Kally's treasured family recipes, most of which are mentioned in the story. *Kate's Secret* (Bluegrass Spirits #2) takes place in horse country outside Midway in Woodford County. Local flavor abounds in both novels.

Kally has been living her own "happily ever after" with her husband of more than 35 years, known affectionately to her readers as Mr. Ray. They have two adult children, a rescued dog, and a rescued cat. And, as her friends and fans know, Kally lives for visits from her adorable grandson, Erik, who was the model for the character Derek in *Jesse's Hideout* and Erik in *Kate's Secret*. (He insisted on having his real name used in the second one!)

Kally enjoys meeting readers at book signings and events throughout North America and is on a mission to meet with at least one reader for a meal, signing, or other event in all 50 states. She's staying closer to home these days, but expects to have KallypsoCon in Virginia or Maryland in 2019. To keep up with upcoming events, check out the Appearances page on her web site! She's always open to having signings in her home state of Kentucky, too!

*For timely updates and much more, sign up for her e-mails or text alerts on her website at **kallypsomasters.com**.*

To contact or engage with Kally, go to:
Facebook (where almost all of her posts are public),
Facebook Author page,
Kally's Patreon Page (for exclusive content/access and serialized stories)
Twitter (@kallypsomasters),
InstaGram (instagram.com/kallypsomasters)
Kally's Web site (KallypsoMasters.com).

And feel free to e-mail Kally at kallypsomasters@gmail.com, or write to her at
Kallypso Masters, PO Box 1183, Richmond, KY 40476-1183

Get your Signed Books & Merchandise in the Kally Store!

Want to own merchandise or personalized, signed paperback copies of any or all of Kallypso Masters' books? New *Bluegrass Spirits* series items will be coming soon, but there's already a line of t-shirts and other items connected to the *Rescue Me Saga* series and Kallypso-Cons. With each order, you'll receive a sports pack filled with Kally's latest FREE items. Kally ships internationally. To shop for these items and much more, go to kallypsomasters.com/kally_swag.

And you can also purchase any of Kally's e-books directly from her now, too! Just click the "Kally's Shop" link for any of the books listed on her website. Or go here for a complete list of available titles. New releases will be published exclusively in Kally's Shop at least two weeks before being available on other retailer sites. kallypsomasters.com/buy-direct

Roar (A Rescue Me Saga Spin-off)

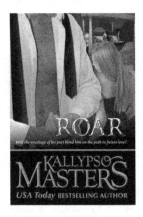

A tragic accident left his beloved wife just beyond his reach, haunting Kristoffer Roar Larson for four years until a chance meeting with Pamela stirs feelings best kept buried. Her assertive alpha personality coupled with her desire to submit and serve fascinates him. Will he allow her presence to shine light once more into the dark corners of his life?

Dr. Pamela Jeffrey thrives on providing medical assistance to those in war-torn corners of the world until a health scare grounds her stateside. While pursuing her deepest secret desire, she encounters Kristoffer, who reluctantly agrees to help prepare her for a future Dom. The bond deepens between them as does her desire for him to be that man in her life, but Kristoffer cannot meet all of her needs. Can she be satisfied without regrets with what he can propose?

As the undeniable connection grows between them, feelings of betrayal take root. How can Pamela convince him he deserves another chance at love? Will Kristoffer be able to fully open himself to the ginger-haired sprite who makes him question everything he once believed? Or will he lose the woman teaching him to live again as surely as he lost the person who first taught him to love?

NOTE: While this book is a standalone, it includes secondary characters from the Rescue Me Saga, including Gunnar Larson, Patrick Gallagher, and V. Grant and there is a scene in the Masters at Arms Club.

Reading Order for the *Rescue Me Saga & Extras*

kallypsomasters.com/books

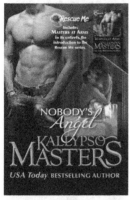

Masters at Arms & Nobody's Angel (Combined Volume)

Nobody's Hero

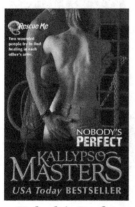

Nobody's Perfect

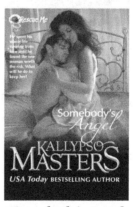

Somebody's Angel

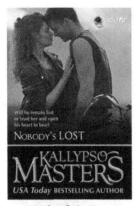

Nobody's Lost

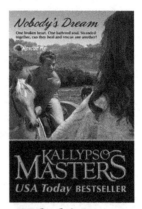

Nobody's Dream

Western Dreams

Somebody's Perfect

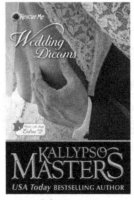

Wedding Dreams

Bluegrass Spirits
(A Supernatural Contemporary Romance series)

From the *USA Today* Best-Selling Author of the *Rescue Me Saga* comes a new Contemporary Romance series with supernatural elements set amidst the many flavors of Kentucky. In *Bluegrass Spirits*, Kallypso Masters distills love and happily ever afters—with a little matchmaking guidance from loved ones on the other side. While there will be updates about earlier couples in each subsequent story, each novel can be enjoyed on its own.

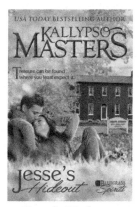

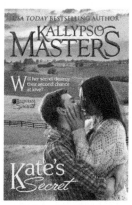

Jesse's Hideout   *Kate's Secret*

Made in the USA
Middletown, DE
09 June 2019